"Was that good for you, *agapi mou?*"

It had been more than good. It had been out of this world. But did Dione want to admit that? What would she be letting herself in for?

"I never knew that making love could be so enervating," she confessed with a wry smile.

Theo's skin glistened in the light from one of the floor lamps, and even in repose he looked imposing. Naked or dressed, aroused or relaxed, he was one hell of an exciting male. She had never thought that when she'd agreed to marry him—had never expected that within a few short days she would be begging him to make love to her.

She had thought that the next twelve months were going to be hell; instead it looked as though she was going to enjoy them!

MARGARET MAYO is a hopeless romantic who loves writing and falls in love with every one of her heroes. It was never her ambition to become an author, although she always loved reading, even to the extent of reading comics out loud to her twin brother when she was eight years old.

She was born in Staffordshire, England, and has lived in the same part of the country ever since. She left school to become a secretary, taking a break to have her two children, Adrian and Tina. Once they were at school she started back to work and planned to further her career by becoming a bilingual secretary. Unfortunately she couldn't speak any languages other than her native English, so she began evening classes. It was at this time that she got the idea for a romantic short story. Margaret, and her mother before her, had always read romances, and to actually be writing one excited her beyond measure. She forgot the languages and now has more than seventy novels to her credit.

Before she became a successful author, Margaret was extremely shy and found it difficult to talk to strangers. For research purposes she forced herself to speak to people from all walks of life, and now says her shyness has gone forever—to a certain degree. She is still happier pouring her thoughts out on paper.

BOUGHT
FOR MARRIAGE
MARGARET MAYO

~ FORCED TO MARRY ~

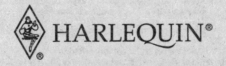

TORONTO • NEW YORK • LONDON
AMSTERDAM • PARIS • SYDNEY • HAMBURG
STOCKHOLM • ATHENS • TOKYO • MILAN • MADRID
PRAGUE • WARSAW • BUDAPEST • AUCKLAND

Recycling programs
for this product may
not exist in your area.

ISBN-13: 978-0-373-52728-1

BOUGHT FOR MARRIAGE

First North American Publication 2009.

Copyright © 2006 by Margaret Mayo.

www.eHarlequin.com

Printed in U.S.A.

BOUGHT
FOR MARRIAGE

CHAPTER ONE

'THEO TSARDIKOS? You expect me to go and beg him for money?' Dione stared at her father in disbelief. 'I can't do it.'

Theodossus Tsardikos was a man to be reckoned with. His name was revered throughout the whole of Greece, and maybe the world for all she knew. He was her father's sworn enemy. He ran a very successful and very luxurious worldwide hotel chain; only the rich and famous could afford to stay there.

Yannis had once tried to persuade Theo to let him franchise his restaurants inside the hotels—the suggestion had been received with raw contempt. Theo made no secret of his dislike of Yannis Keristari. And Dione couldn't blame him.

Yannis slumped back against his pillow. 'Then this will be the end of me.'

'I think,' said Phrosini, with a worried glance at her husband before looking pleadingly at her stepdaughter, 'that your father meant you to think about it. Let's go home. We'll come back later and talk about this.'

As they left his hospital room Dione glanced over her shoulder at the man who had been such a big controlling influence on her life and found it hard to believe that he was asking her to do this. She'd done most things; she'd been the best daughter she could under the circumstances, but begging for money? From his arch-enemy? How insulting could he be?

Her mind flew back twenty-four hours to when she'd received the phone call from a distraught Phrosini saying he was ill and was asking for her.

'Of course I'll come. I'll be on the next available flight.'

Dione turned to her mother, an anxious expression on her lovely face. 'I need to return home. Father's in hospital; he's had a heart attack.'

Jeannie's hand flew to her mouth. 'Oh, dear! Naturally you must go. I'll tell Chris for you. I do hope Yannis will be OK.'

A magnanimous thought after the way he had treated her, decided Dione. But that was her mother; she rarely thought ill of anyone. She was quiet and undemanding and Dione privately thought that she let people walk all over her. Not that she would ever tell her parent that; she loved her too dearly.

To her dismay there were no available seats on flights to Athens until the next day, but at least it gave her the opportunity to tell Chris herself.

'I'll come with you,' he said at once when he saw her that evening. 'I can't let my fiancée go through this alone.'

He'd said it so proudly that Dione felt guilty. She had been planning to take Chris to Greece to meet her father, to get his approval for their wedding, but not under these circumstances. The shock of discovering that she was going to marry an Englishman would probably kill her father altogether.

Yannis was Greek through and through. Very proud, very traditional, and it was his ambition that Dione should marry one of his own kind. Dione, though, had other ideas. She wanted to escape her father's domineering nature and the only way she could do it, as far as she could see, was to marry and settle in England.

She had met Christopher Donovan on one of her frequent visits to the UK and when he proposed she had thought about it long and hard before finally accepting. It wasn't that she didn't love Chris, she did, but it was his love for her that she wasn't so sure about.

He had gone out with her on the rebound from a previous relationship and assured her that it was all over. But she had heard from a third party only the other day that the girl still hankered after him and that he had been seen with her. She had tackled Chris and he had looked startled at first, and then said that there was no truth in it.

'I think it would be best if I went alone,' she said to him now. 'My father's too ill to meet strangers.'

'You're probably right,' he agreed. 'You will phone me?'

'Naturally.'

The plane landed at Athens Airport and Dione strode through the arrivals lounge, a stunningly attractive woman in a cream trouser suit teamed with a chocolate-coloured top. Her long blue-black hair brushed her shoulders sensuously with each step that she took in her high-heeled sandals, causing many a male head to turn.

Dione was oblivious. She headed for the taxi rank, not expecting anyone to meet her, but surprised and pleased to see her stepmother.

'Phrosini, how nice of you! I didn't anticipate this.' She hugged the woman warmly, easily falling into her second language. 'Shouldn't you be with Father? How is he? Is he any better?'

Phrosini was short and plump but extremely beautiful, and it was easy to see why her father had fallen in love with her. She was as different from Dione's mother as it was possible for two people to be. His first marriage had been a definite mistake. They had probably loved each other to begin with, surmised Dione, but her mother had been too weak to stand up to his bossy nature. Phrosini could handle him beautifully without him even realising it.

'There's no change,' answered Phrosini. 'Except that he's excited you're coming. He really is ill, Dione. I'm worried to death.'

'Why didn't you let me know sooner?'

Phrosini grimaced apologetically. 'I didn't want to spoil your holiday. I know how much you enjoy being in England with your mother. At first I thought he'd recover quickly, but he didn't and he started asking for you. I couldn't reason with him.'

They drove straight to the hospital. 'I'm sorry, I know you'll want to freshen up, but your father's anxious to see you,' explained Phrosini.

And when Dione walked into Yannis' room she was shocked by his appearance. He wasn't a tall man, had always been slim and dapper, but he'd lost so much weight that he looked gaunt to the point of danger, his skin grey and drawn, and he was hooked up to a host of machines that monitored his every function.

'Dione!' he croaked. 'You're here!'

She crossed the room and hugged him. 'Yes, Father. How are you feeling? It's so naughty of you not to let me know you were ill.'

He stroked her hand. 'Didn't want to worry you, child.'

'So what brought on your heart attack?' she wanted to know. 'I thought you had the constitution of an ox.'

'Not any more.' Yannis glanced at Phrosini. 'You tell her,' he said in a hoarse whisper.

'Tell me what?'

Phrosini closed her eyes, and when she opened them again Dione saw a wealth of worry. 'Your father's business is failing—badly.'

'What?' Dione frowned. How could that be? Yannis had inherited a restaurant from his father and turned it into a successful chain. There had been no talk of it losing money.

'Trade's been dropping off considerably,' Phrosini informed her, her voice quiet and desperate. 'It needs a big injection of money for a facelift and your father hasn't got it. He's paying out more than he gets in. We're almost bankrupt, Dione.'

Dione was shocked but not truly surprised. She had trained in England as an interior designer, hoping to move there permanently and get a job, but Yannis had insisted she work for him. She spent her time travelling between the different restaurants, renovating where necessary—but always under Yannis' eagle eye.

He was a pure traditionalist, so old-fashioned that he would never let her impose any of her modern ideas. He said traditional values gave the restaurants atmosphere and would not be shifted. Dione had privately had her doubts. People wanted modern and lively these days. They didn't want to live in the past.

'This is awful,' she said. 'I had no idea.'

'Nor did I,' confessed Phrosini. 'Your father kept it from me—and as a result he's in here.' She put her hand over her husband's and squeezed gently. 'You're a very stubborn man, you know that.'

Yannis grimaced. 'It's all up to you now, daughter,' he said quietly, looking at Dione. 'You're my only hope.'

'Me?' Dione touched her fingers to her chest. 'How can I help? I don't have that sort of money.' She really didn't have a lot of savings. Her father paid her the minimum wage he would have paid anyone else and it all went on her flights to England.

'I want you to go and ask Theo Tsardikos for a loan,' he explained in a hoarse, breathless whisper. It clearly cost him to even talk. 'He'll drive a hard bargain, I know that, but if anyone can do it you can.'

'I know it's a lot to ask of you,' said Phrosini now as they sat and drank coffee back at home in their beautiful villa and talked about Yannis. 'But you're our only hope, your father's only hope. If he doesn't get this money his life will be over. He won't have the will to live. He's dying now. The doctors are doing all they can but…' She let her voice fade away and even she looked pale and ill.

'Surely there must be some other way?' pondered Dione. She wasn't afraid of Theo Tsardikos, even though he was a powerful man; it would be more embarrassing than anything else. 'What about the banks?'

'They're closing in on him.'

And Dione knew that he didn't have any friends who would help. There were not many people who liked her father; he was a tyrant of the highest order, and she had more reason than most to hate him after the way he had treated her mother. But he was her blood after all and though she found it hard to forgive him she loved him. She kept the peace mainly for her emotionally vulnerable mother's sake, not knowing what he might say or do to her if she got on the wrong side of him.

Jeannie and Yannis had divorced sixteen years ago. When their marriage broke up he had moved back to his native Greece, taking Dione with him. Reluctantly he had let her visit her mother during school holidays. Now she spent as much time in England as she possibly could, and had been on the second week of a month's visit when she had got the call.

'It's a lot to ask of me.'

'I know,' said Phrosini.

Dione had grown close to her stepmother and loved her dearly but at this moment in time she wished that she wasn't asking the impossible of her. Phrosini had never had any children of her own, much to Yannis' disappointment because he'd always wanted sons, and so she looked upon Dione as her own daughter.

Now Dione faced the little Greek woman with compassion in her eyes. 'It looks as though I have no choice.'

And when they went back to the hospital to tell her father Dione was glad that she'd made the decision. He looked if possible even more sallow and ill than earlier. He lay in his bed, his breathing laboured, but as soon as he heard her news he smiled and a light appeared in his eyes.

'Thank you, Dione. Thank you from the bottom of my rotten heart.' And he took her hands and squeezed them.

Dione took a deep breath as she stood outside the door and prepared to face the legendary Theo Tsardikos.

Her father's life depended on her succeeding.

But how easy would it be, when they were total enemies?

CHAPTER TWO

THEO looked with interest at the woman standing in front of him. He was aware that Yannis Keristari had a daughter but he had never met her and was pleasantly surprised.

She was tall and slender and very fine looking, somewhere in her twenties, he imagined. She wore a grey jacket with a matching pencil-slim skirt and high-heeled shoes. The jacket was fastened to just above her breasts and a gold pendant dangled enticingly close to her cleavage. He couldn't help wondering why she had chosen to fasten it so demurely on such a warm day, and it amused him to assume that she wore nothing beneath.

Her eyes were dark and sloe-shaped with a fan of thick lashes, her nose straight and small, and her mouth—was delicious. He forced himself to look from it. She was nothing like her father, which came as something of a surprise. And totally unlike any other Greek woman he'd met. He was fascinated. Even more so than with the reason she was here.

Which had yet to be revealed.

Clearly Keristari had sent her. Theo had heard through the grapevine that Yannis Keristari's business was in trouble. Had his daughter's visit anything to do with it? Perhaps he was offering to sell him his restaurants?

He showed his visitor to a seat, not once taking his eyes off her, and waited for her to speak. She was graceful in her movements and smelled like a dream.

'Mr Tsardikos.'

'Please, call me Theo.'

'This isn't a social visit,' she declared with a delightful toss of her head that revealed a long, slender neck simply begging to be kissed. Theo sat down behind his desk to stop himself from advancing towards her. 'Maybe,' he growled. 'But there's no need for formalities, especially when you're the daughter of an old...acquaintance of mine.' He'd been about to say enemy, but realised that this could get her back up before she'd even given her reason for being here. 'Would you like coffee? I can get someone to—'

'No!'

It was an instant decision. She was clearly on a mission and wanted to get it over with. 'So how can I help you?' He folded his arms, allowing his eyes to half close as he studied her intently. He could feel a stirring in his groin that shocked him to the core. This was the daughter of a man he hadn't the faintest admiration for. He should be totally indifferent to her. So why wasn't he?

'My father needs money.'

He felt quite sure she hadn't intended to blurt it out like that because a tell-tale colouring to her skin belied her cool outer image. But he was glad that she had because he now knew where he stood. His mind had run to the fact that her father could be offering him first refusal on the business. But money! How much had it cost Keristari to send her here?

'Is that so?' he asked with cool indifference. He had no intention in the world of helping this man out.

Dione nodded. 'He believes that you might be able to help him.'

Theo wanted to tell her straight away that he wouldn't. Keristari was a bully of the highest order and most definitely not a man to do business with.

But he didn't want to let Dione go yet. He was fascinated. She was quite the sexiest woman he had met in a long time. There was something refreshingly different about her. It was as though she had no idea of her own sexuality. How he would like to introduce her to it.

'Why ask me?' he asked, leaning back in his chair, his hands linked behind his head. 'Why not his bank?'

'I think he's in too deep for that,' admitted Dione. 'He says you're his only hope. He's counting on it.'

Dione saw the disbelief on Theo Tsardikos' face, the hint of anger quickly suppressed, and knew that her mission was doomed to failure. But she still needed to try. The image of her father lying helpless in hospital flashed in front of her mind's eye. Much as she feared him, much as she sometimes despised him, she couldn't bear to see him so ill and worried.

'He's counting on it!' repeated Theo disbelievingly, dragging dark brows together over velvety brown eyes. 'Why would he ask me, the man he probably hates more than anyone else in the world, for money? Unless, of course, he's exhausted all his other options.'

'I don't know,' said Dione, her eyes steady on this

tall, undeniably handsome man with a shock of dark hair that looked as though he constantly ran his fingers through it. 'I didn't know anything about it until yesterday. I've been visiting my mother in England.'

'So Phrosini isn't your birth mother?' he enquired, sharp interest on his face.

Dione shook her head. She wished he wasn't quite so good-looking. She wished his eyes wouldn't rake over her as though he wanted to take her to bed.

'That explains why you look nothing like either of your parents.'

'Which has nothing to do with the reason I'm here,' declared Dione heatedly. She certainly wasn't here to discuss her parentage.

He allowed himself to smile and his very even white teeth looked predatory in her heightened state. Like a wolf about to pounce, she thought. This was a man she had to watch closely. He looked relaxed leaning back in his chair, his shirt collar undone, but his mind was as sharp as a razor.

'Your father's using you, you do know that?' he pointed out. 'Like he uses everyone he comes into contact with. The best thing you can do, Dione—do you mind if I call you Dione?—is to go right back and tell him the answer's no.'

Dione drew in a pained breath. What a heartless brute the man was. 'You haven't even asked how much he wants,' she retorted, her back stiff, her eyes sparking resentment.

'It's immaterial,' he said. 'I wouldn't lend your father one euro, let alone thousands of them, which I presume is the kind of amount he'd want. What's happened?'

Dione shrugged. 'All I know is that he's nearly bankrupt.'

'Bad management,' drawled Theo uncaringly.

'So that's your final answer?' she snapped, her heart dipping so low it almost touched her shoes.

Theo leaned back in his chair, a smile playing on well-shaped lips, and an unfathomable gleam in his eyes. 'There could be another solution.'

Dione's heart leapt with hope.

'I could save your father's business—on one condition.'

'And that is?' asked Dione eagerly.

There was a long pause before he answered, a space of time when his eyes raked insolently over her body, sending a shiver of unease through her limbs. But she didn't let him see it; she sat still, her hands folded primly in her lap, and waited to hear what he had to say.

'That you become my wife.'

The shock of his suggestion couldn't have been greater. This man was a stranger to her, as she was to him, and yet he was talking about marriage! Was he out of his mind? Would he lend her father money just to get his hands on her? What sort of a monster was he? Dione shivered as rivers of ice raced down her spine.

She jumped to her feet and glared. 'That is the most outrageous suggestion I've ever heard. What makes you think I'd marry a total stranger?'

A faint, insolent smile curved his mouth. 'I thought you had your father's best interests at heart. Otherwise why would you be here?'

'I do,' she admitted, 'but that doesn't include giving myself away to you.' The man had no idea what he was asking. He was probably a fantastic lover with years of experience, but it meant nothing to her. She didn't know the first thing about him. And nor did she want to if these were his tactics.

'It's your choice,' he said, as simply as if they were discussing a normal business proposition. 'If your answer's no then we have nothing else to discuss.'

'Of course my answer's no,' she spat at him. 'What do you take me for?' And with that she whirled on her heel and stormed out of the room.

His mocking voice called after her. 'I'll be waiting should you change your mind.'

'Then you'll wait a lifetime,' she hissed beneath her breath.

Dione didn't go straight to the hospital; she was far too wound up for that. She had taken a taxi to Theo's office but now decided to walk. Even then she took a circuitous route and by the time she did reach the hospital she was almost able to laugh at Theo Tsardikos' suggestion.

But her father didn't laugh. 'You could do worse,' he said. 'I've always wanted you to marry a proud Greek male and Tsardikos is as good as they come.'

Praise indeed coming from her father, thought Dione.

'I've been so afraid that on one of your trips to England you'll fall in love. It would break my heart.'

It was on the tip of Dione's tongue to tell him about Chris, but at the last moment she decided against it. Yannis' health was so bad that such an admission might finish him off altogether. In fact he looked even worse today that he had yesterday. His breathing was laboured and his skin a ghostly yellow and Phrosini hovered, not knowing what to do to help her beloved husband.

'I can't marry a complete stranger,' Dione said miserably.

'Not even for me?' demanded Yannis in a rough, angry voice. 'Not even though my life and my livelihood depend on it? What sort of a daughter are you?'

He made Dione feel guilty, but even so she stuck to her guns. 'I'd be prostituting myself.'

'With Tsardikos? He's an exciting male. Half the female population of Greece are after him. You'll be the envy of thousands.' And then he slumped in his chair and hardly seemed to be breathing.

Phrosini beckoned her out of the room. 'We must leave him for a while,' she said.

'Don't you know he's asking the impossible?' asked Dione, as they made their way to the hospital restaurant. 'I haven't said anything to my father, and I don't want you to either, but there's a man in England I've promised to marry.'

'Oh, Dione, why didn't you say?' Her stepmother was full of concern.

'How could I when my father's so ill, and more especially after what he's just said?'

'And this boy, you love him?'

'Of course.' But Dione's face gave away the fact that it wasn't exactly going to be a marriage made in heaven.

'You're doing it because you don't want your father to arrange a marriage for you?' she asked intuitively.

Dione nodded faintly, her lips clamped together. When it was put to her like that she realised it was probably true. The love she felt for Chris wasn't like the stuff you read about, but she had been happy enough—until she heard that he'd been seen with his ex-girlfriend!

'Oh, Dione, is that really the answer? I don't want you to be unhappy like I was with my first husband, like your mother was.'

'I'd be happier with Chris than Theo Tsardikos,' said Dione quietly.

'Theo's a good man. His offer is a lifeline to your father. In fact it might save his life. The doctors are very fearful today.' There were tears in Phrosini's eyes. 'And if he doesn't recover...well, your father's always wanted me to carry on the business if anything should happen to him.'

Meaning she would be letting them both down. Put like that, how could she refuse? Dione breathed in deeply, closed her eyes, then took the plunge, hating herself for it but knowing it was something she had to do.

'OK—I'll—marry him.' Her words floated in the air like a storm cloud threatening to bear down and drown her in a black deluge of unhappiness.

Phrosini hugged her tightly, tears streaming down her cheeks. 'My precious child.'

There was nothing precious about it, thought Dione, but she made up her mind there and then that Theo Tsardikos would not get it all his own way. This marriage would be on her terms.

He was savagely handsome, quite the best-looking man she'd ever seen—tall, with a perfectly honed body and long-fingered, well-manicured hands. It was one of the first things she'd noticed about him. But it didn't mean that she would eagerly jump into his bed. Quite the opposite! She would be a good and dutiful wife in every other respect. She would cook for him, entertain for him, accompany him whenever necessary, but nothing more.

Maybe this was what he wanted her to be—a good hostess? A man in his position would need someone at his side on special occasions.

And who was she trying to kid?

She had seen the way he looked at her, the way his eyes had raked insolently over her body, and she had known what he was thinking, even though she'd done her very best to ignore it.

Already she was beginning to lament her decision but her father was overjoyed when they went back to tell him, his eyes brightening and becoming alert and interested. 'My darling daughter! You won't regret this, I promise you.'

Dione wasn't so sure.

She spent a sleepless night worrying about it, telling herself there was still time to back out, but then recalling her father's pleasure. How could she deny him his dying wish?

As Dione sat outside Theo Tsardikos' office for the second time in the same number of days her heart leapt with alarming violence. This was going to be the hardest thing she had ever done. Giving herself to a man she didn't know was crazy. She had to be insane to do it.

And the man in question was taking great delight in keeping her waiting!

And the longer Dione waited the more irritated she became, until at last she jumped to her feet and prepared to leave. She couldn't do this, not even for her father's sake. No one knew the courage it had taken her to come here this morning; courage that was fast deserting her.

'Leaving, are we?'

Dione spun round at the sound of a deep, gravelly voice and looked into a pair of amused dark eyes. 'I'd begun to think you didn't want to see me. I've sat here for twenty minutes.'

'I'm a busy man, Dione. And you did arrive without an appointment. But now I'm all yours. Do come in.' And he touched a hand to her arm as he led her into his office.

It was a large, airy room with a wooden floor and pale grey walls hung with photographs of his various hotels. His desk was in front of the massive window with its views over Athens, and in one corner was a trio of armchairs. Against another wall was a series of bookcases. It was clean and clinical and efficient. Like the man himself.

She headed towards the desk, prepared to sit in the seat opposite him, as she had before, but instead he steered her towards the armchairs. 'We'll be more comfortable here.'

Dione did not want to be comfortable; she wanted to say what she had to say and get out quickly. Not the right sort of thought when Theo was her prospective husband—though actually she was hoping that he'd had a change of heart. A hope that was quickly dashed when he flashed his wolfish teeth.

'Can I presume that the reason you're here is to declare that you'll marry me after all?'

Two pairs of brown eyes met and warred, and Dione was the first to look away. 'I'd like to be able to say no,' she snapped, ignoring the stammer of her heart. This man was lethal. Deadly attractive but a danger all the same.

'You're a free agent.' The words were tossed lightly and dismissively into the air and Dione gained the impression that he couldn't care less. That this was all some sort of game to him.

'Meaning *you've* changed *your* mind?' she enquired sharply, mentally crossing her fingers that this was so.

'Not at all.' It was a simple, matter-of-fact answer; he was giving her no help whatsoever. In fact he was enjoying her discomfort.

'In that case,' she said in a voice not much above a whisper, 'I'll do as you ask.'

'I'm sorry, I can't hear you.'

Damn the man! A satisfied smile played about his sculpted lips and his eyes were filled with amusement. She felt pretty sure that he had heard. He just wanted to hear her say it again. He liked seeing her squirm.

'I said, I'll do as you ask.' There, was that loud enough for him? She'd projected the words as though she was throwing a missile, hoping they'd smash into his face and wipe some of the pleasure off it.

No such luck! His smile widened and deepened and he leaned forward and took her hands into his. 'There, that wasn't so bad, was it?'

Dione huffed and said nothing.

'You're not happy?'

'No, I'm not.'

'But I'm guessing your father's delirious?'

'He was pleased, yes.'

'He must really have hit rock-bottom.'

Dione flashed furious dark eyes at him. 'He has, and he's in hospital fighting for his life because of it.'

Theo frowned. 'I didn't know that.'

'There's a lot about my father you don't know.'

'And a lot I do,' he growled. 'He's unscrupulous. I bet he had no hesitation in saying you should marry me. How he could have produced a daughter like you I don't know.'

'How do you know I'm not unscrupulous too?' she riposted, wishing she could jump up and run. This was the most humiliating experience of her life.

'I'm good at reading people.'

'How do you know that if I marry you I won't take you for every penny you've got?' she slammed at him.

'Because I've already had a contract drawn up. I—'

'You've what?' interjected Dione in horror. 'You were that sure I'd say yes?'

'Absolutely,' he agreed, stretching out his long legs and linking his hands behind his head.

He looked so relaxed she wanted to take a swipe at him, knock some of that pleasure off his damnably handsome face. 'You bastard!'

Theo's well-shaped brows rose. 'Tut, tut, Dione! Here was I, thinking you were a lady.'

'You bring out the worst in me,' she savaged.

'It's not all I plan to bring out in you,' he said with a cruel smile. 'Let's get down to business. You *are* here to say that you will marry me in return for me bailing your father out of trouble?'

Dione swallowed hard, ignored the little voice inside her head that told her to get up and run, ignored the thought of a nice, safe English marriage to Chris Donovan, and nodded.

His lips curved in satisfaction. 'I never thought I'd say this, but your father's a very lucky man, do you know that? Not many girls would do this for their father. Pray tell me, why do you love him so much? Or is it perhaps because you fear him?' He saw the flicker in her eyes and nodded. 'He has you in the same stranglehold as everyone else. I pity you, Dione, having a father like that, though I applaud what you are doing.'

'Only because it's in your favour,' she snorted, deeply annoyed that he had summed up the situation so correctly. Did everyone know that her father was a control freak?

'As I said, I've had a contract drawn up; all you have to do is sign it.' He rose from the chair and strode across to his desk.

Dione watched, her heart aching with a pain she had never felt before. Sorrow, anger, despair. Not that she let Theo see any of this. When he returned to his seat she lifted her chin and sat that little bit straighter. 'I have a few stipulations of my own before I sign anything.'

Dark brows rose. 'Are you in any position?'

'I think I am.'

He lifted broad shoulders. 'I beg to differ on that point, but go ahead. Unless, of course, you'd like to read my contract first? You might be pleasantly surprised.'

Dione privately doubted it, but maybe she ought to take a look before she jumped in with her own criteria.

It wasn't a long document, but in essence it gave him full power to treat her as he liked in return for helping her father out of his financial troubles. *To become my wife in every sense for as long as I desire,* were the words that sprang out from the page.

Not on his life!

She thrust it back at him. 'No! Absolutely no!'

'To what exactly?' he enquired insouciantly. He had clearly expected her denial and was now going to take great pleasure in having her spell it out to him.

'I will not go to bed with you.' When all her friends had been sleeping around Dione had kept her virginity,

saving it for the man she would eventually marry—
someone she loved and respected. She had thought
Chris that man until very recently. But she was definitely not giving herself to Theo Tsardikos. Not ever!
'Nor will I remain married to you for longer than one
year,' she added stormily. 'In all other respects I will be
your wife.'

'There are no other respects,' he growled. 'A wife is
a wife. A wife spends time in her husband's bed. A wife
pleasures her man.'

'A wife also cooks and cleans and entertains.'

'I have people to do that sort of thing,' he answered
dismissively. 'It's a bed companion I want and I think
you'll fit the bill admirably. You're beautiful, you're
spirited, you're caring. What more could a man ask for?
But—maybe I can agree to your condition.'

Theo smiled to himself. It had never been his intention
for them to sleep in separate beds. On the other hand it
would be interesting trying to change her mind. In fact,
the chase could be as enjoyable as the kill.

He had wanted her from the first second he saw her.
She was quite the most striking and intriguing woman
he'd ever met. He had dreamed about her last night, and
what an exciting lover she had been! If dream became
actuality, however... His gut twisted at the very thought.

In one respect he felt sorry for Dione, and the
pressure Keristari had put on her. He wanted to make
their sham of a marriage reality; he wanted her to learn
to love him as a woman should love a man, not to marry
him under duress and out of loyalty to her father.
Keristari was a man whom no one liked except for his

very loyal wife. Phrosini deserved a medal for putting up with his bullying ways.

What had happened, he wondered, between him and Dione's mother? Clearly she hadn't tolerated his dictatorial manner; she had got out while she could. And good for her! Maybe Dione would tell him the story one day.

'So do you intend drawing up another contract?' she asked him now, her chin determinedly high, her lovely, liquid brown eyes revealing her distaste of what was about to happen.

Lord, he wanted to take her into his arms and assure her that everything would be all right. That he wasn't an ogre, that he wouldn't hurt her. And that he admired what she was doing. But that wasn't part of the game.

He was frankly appalled that she would marry him simply to please her father and drag him out of the mire he'd got himself into. It was misplaced loyalty as far as he was concerned.

Naturally he was sympathetic towards Keristari's illness, but that didn't change him from the bullying tyrant he'd always been. And even in his illness he was controlling all those around him. It was no way to behave towards your loved ones. He did not deserve their devotion.

He was so angry with the man that his tone was sharply aggressive when he answered her question. 'Naturally. I will have it ready for your signature this afternoon.'

Dione's head jerked as she stared at him wild-eyed. 'So soon?'

'Why wait?' he asked smoothly. 'I don't imagine your father will want to drag this thing out. If he's in

as much trouble as you say he'll want the money now.
But no marriage, no funding! Shall we set the wedding
for Sunday? Is two days enough for you to get your
head round it?'

CHAPTER THREE

THEO almost laughed when he saw the consternation on Dione's face.

'Two days?' she choked. 'You can't wait to get your hands on me, is that it? Damn you, Theo Tsardikos! Damn you to hell.'

Lord, wasn't she gorgeous when she was angry? He felt his testosterone levels rising and it was all he could do not to drag her into his arms and kiss her senseless. 'I was thinking of your father's money,' he answered, amazing himself at his coolness when inside he was on fire.

'I bet you were,' she snapped. 'I've seen the way you look at me. But don't forget, we shall have a piece of paper forbidding you to touch. And heaven help you if you renege.'

What a spirited person she was. What an exciting woman. His male hormones danced all over the place. 'I wouldn't dream of it,' he said slowly, levelly. 'Anything in that direction will have to come from you.'

'Then you'll wait till hell freezes over,' she tossed cruelly.

He folded his arms across his chest, dropped his head

to one side and studied her. 'You're amazing, do you know that?'

'Amazing?' she scoffed. 'I'm simply telling you how it is. This is a business contract. Nothing more, nothing less, and you'd best remember it.'

'I will remember,' he told her. Whatever happened between him and this intriguing young lady, whether they made a success of the marriage—wishful thinking—or it failed abysmally—more like it—it would stay in his memory for the rest of his life.

'Good,' she snapped, standing up, and with another flash of her lovely dark eyes she headed for the door.

He did not want to let her go yet—he wanted her to stay, to talk some more; he wanted to get to know this gorgeous creature better. But sanity told him to take things easy. In any case, she had to come back to sign the new contract. His lips quirked at the pleasure of seeing her again so soon. Perhaps at his home rather than here, where they could talk longer, get to know each other better.

And then on Sunday—she would be his!

He had a lot to organise, a lot of arrangements to make. No time to detain her. He walked to the door and bade her goodbye. 'Till later, Dione. I'll ring you when the contract's ready. Will you be home?'

Dione glared into his face. 'I have no idea.'

'Then give me your mobile number.' He half expected her to refuse; was surprised when she wrote it down without argument. He tucked the slip of paper into his pocket and held out his hand. She ignored it, spinning on her heel and rushing out of the office as though all the hounds in hell were chasing her.

Theo smiled to himself. He was rarely short of female company but no woman had appealed to him as Dione Keristari did now. She had turned up under the most distressing of situations; she'd been forced to approach him by her demanding father, but beneath her hostility, beneath the fear she had felt when confronting him, was a beautiful woman simply waiting to be loved.

Dione marched out of the office building with her mind in torment. Theo wanted from her exactly what she'd feared. A wife in every sense of the word! Thank goodness she'd been able to talk him around; though in actual fact she wasn't totally convinced that he would keep his word. He was the sort of guy who if you gave him an inch would take a mile.

Not wanting to go back to the hospital yet, she took herself into the village where they lived near Athens, sat outside a café and ordered coffee.

It was hard to believe that Theo Tsardikos had expected her to become his wife in every sense of the word right from the moment the ring was put on her finger. Had he no idea what it would be like to let a complete stranger make love to her? She couldn't even visualise letting it happen.

No, if he didn't stick to his side of the bargain, she would walk away from the marriage regardless. And if Tsardikos demanded his money back then her father would have to find someone else to dig him out of the mire he'd got himself into. It was as simple as that.

Or so she told herself. In fact it wasn't. She couldn't let her father down. She had let herself down by agreeing to this marriage, but if Theo drew up the contract in accordance with her request then she couldn't see anything going wrong. He was a man of his word, she felt sure, and, although he might enjoy goading her, he wouldn't force her to do anything she didn't want to do.

How long she sat there drinking coffee Dione wasn't sure. A few people she knew paused to pass the time of day but by and large she sat there alone and tried to digest the very big step that she was going to take.

She had to phone her mother, of course. And Chris. But it wasn't something she was looking forward to. Procrastination would be the name of the game here. Maybe after the marriage? When it was a *fait accompli* and they could do nothing about it. Was that too awful of her? But how could she tell them right at this very minute, when she had never felt so vulnerable in her life?

She had been driven into a corner by two scheming men, both of them as bad as the other. Twelve months was a lifetime when you weren't happy. It was a prison sentence. Her head spun and she sat there for hours until Spiros, the owner, came to ask whether she was all right.

'Dione, you sit here so long. You look very troubled.'

She had known him virtually all her life and smiled wanly. 'My father's ill,' she declared. 'I'm worried about him.' If only it were that simple.

'I am sorry. Please—give him my best wishes. I hope he is better soon.'

'Me too, Spiros. Me too.'

The phone call came sooner than she expected and her heart jerked into overdrive at the sound of Theo's deep, warm voice.

'Dione, it is time. I will pick you up. Where are you?'

'No!' She almost spat the word. 'There's no need. I will come to your office.'

'I'm at home,' he told her, and Dione's heart sank.

'You—you want me to come to your house?' How awful would that be!

'I thought you would be more relaxed.'

'If you think I'll ever be relaxed marrying an arrogant beast like you then you're very much mistaken,' she told him boldly.

Theo laughed. 'What a charming vocabulary you have.' And then his voice hardened. 'I repeat, where are you?'

Best not get on the wrong side of him, at least not until the money was safely in her father's bank account, thought Dione. 'I'm at Spiros' Café. Do you know it?'

'No.'

She hadn't thought he would. It was not the sort of place he would use. 'Give me your address and I'll find my way there,' she suggested coolly.

Theo made some sort of disagreeable grunting noise. 'Take a taxi. I'll see you soon.'

His villa was as large and impressive as she had imagined it would be, with the usual white stucco walls and red roofs but approached by a long drive and guarded like a fortress. She let the taxi drop her off at the gates and didn't buzz to announce her arrival until the vehicle had gone. Then she walked up the drive, lined on each side by olive trees, and saw Theo waiting for her.

He had changed from his business suit into a pair of casual trousers and a white shirt that stretched across a broad, powerful chest previously hidden to her enquiring eyes. His arms were muscular and tanned and he looked like a man who wasn't afraid of hard work. He also looked younger and less formidable but Dione knew that she must still be wary of him. This wasn't a social visit; this was business with a capital B.

Never had Dione felt more like turning and running. In two days' time this would be her home. She would live here with Theo; she would be his wife in the eyes of the law and every one of his acquaintances. But not in her eyes; never in her eyes! The marriage would never be consummated.

It was too embarrassing by far to ever tell anyone the real reason she was marrying Theo. For twelve months she would act as she'd never acted before, she would carry out her father's wishes, but she would walk away at the end of it with her head held high, confident in the knowledge that Theo Tsardikos had not had his evil way with her.

The villa was spacious and airy and expensive—and beautifully furnished. She fell in love with it straight away. Although it was large it was not pretentious. Theo, she hated to admit, had excellent taste. 'Why, this is lovely,' she said, unable to help herself.

'Wait until you see outside,' he answered, leading her through the villa and looking pleased by her enthusiasm.

And there in front of them was the ocean. Tiered down to it was a series of swimming pools and sun decks, some sheltered by palms and other plants, others bearing the full brunt of the hot summer sun. It was paradise.

'You have a perfect home,' she told him reluctantly.

'And it's going to be your home as well,' he said, turning to face her. 'Do you still think you're getting a bad deal?'

'As far as my emotions go, yes,' she told him truthfully. 'But as far as my senses are concerned, this is sheer heaven.' Her own home with her father was very beautiful but it would never match up to this. They had a pool, yes, but quite a small one in comparison, and they certainly didn't have a sea view. Her father would be as jealous as hell if he only knew.

And she must remember that it was for her father that she was doing this. He was the one forcing her to live in this idyllic spot. Maybe it was wise if she didn't tell him.

'I'm glad you approve; it's half the battle. Let's get down to business, shall we?'

They returned indoors and in his study, a cool, air-conditioned room with very little in the way of furniture apart from a hugely functional desk and a couple of chairs, he handed her a sheet of paper.

Dione sat and read it and she was satisfied. He was demanding nothing from her that she was not prepared to give, apart from her time. The contract was to run for twelve months from the day they married, and after that she was free to leave. He would divorce her without question and he would deposit into her father's bank account, the day after their marriage, whatever sum of money Yannis needed to build up his business again.

It was a very generous agreement under the circumstances, thought Dione. Theo was getting nothing out of it and it was costing him dear. There had to be a catch in it somewhere. But she read it through three times and it was all very straightforward. She took the pen he offered and signed. Theo countersigned.

And it was all done.

On Sunday she would become his wife.

All she hoped was that her father appreciated exactly what she was doing for him.

* * *

The day dawned with a cloudless blue sky and a hot sun powering down on them. Dione had still not telephoned her mother. She wanted to protect her parent, not let her worry and fear that in some incalculable way Yannis still had a hold over her. Jeannie never said much about him but Dione knew that she sometimes feared that her past would come back to haunt her.

And Dione had not seen Theo again either. A special delivery had revealed a stunning wedding dress in ivory silk and every accessory she would need to go with it. Dione guessed there had been some collusion with Phrosini because how could he have possibly known her size?

But she did not question her stepmother; she saw no point in it. The deed was done. She was to become Theo's wife and that was that. Personally she would have worn an oyster-coloured suit that was her favourite; now she was being forced to dress up as though it were a real wedding and she and Theo were very much in love.

Through the grapevine she'd heard that a whole host of guests had been invited. They were getting married in the hospital chapel so that Yannis could be present. No doubt, thought Dione bitterly, he wanted to make doubly sure that she wouldn't run away at the last minute.

Which was extremely tempting.

It was all very emotional and when finally, at a few minutes past three, she became Theo's wife, Dione burst into tears. Everyone cheered and clapped and no one knew, except for Phrosini and Yannis, that it was not a real wedding.

'You're very beautiful, Mrs Tsardikos,' said Theo softly as they walked out of the chapel that had been decked with a myriad of flowers tied with soft satin ribbons and looked charming.

'I don't feel it,' she said, so quietly that no one else heard. 'I feel a fraud.'

'I won't allow you to say that,' he announced curtly, taking her hand and squeezing it. 'To the outside world you are the beautiful girl who has captured Theo Tsardikos' heart. You will become quite famous, *agapi mou.*'

Dione groaned inwardly. She hadn't realised how much of a stir Theo's marriage would cause. She had hoped—she had prayed, in fact—that it would be a quiet affair, but the guests had poured into the hospital, overflowing into corridors, and congratulations had fallen thick and fast.

The reception was being held at Theo's villa and they made their way now in streams of cars that ferried people across the city. The gardens and terraces were decked with flowers and garlands, a band played and exquisite food was served.

Theo made a speech saying what a lucky man he was and Dione blushed her way through it. Theo's parents told her that she had made their son a very happy man, and his sister, Alexandra, couldn't quite believe it either.

'I never thought that Theo would marry again after what happened,' she said to Dione. 'In fact, he swore he wouldn't. You must be someone very special to get him to change his mind.'

CHAPTER FOUR

THEO had been married before! Dione stared at Alexandra in disbelief.

'He hasn't told you, has he?' enquired his sister. 'I'm actually not too surprised because he never talks about it. Not ever. It's as though he's shut what happened completely out of his life.'

'So—what did happen?' questioned Dione. For some reason her heart was thumping wildly.

'Maybe I ought to let Theo himself tell you,' said Alexandra, looking suddenly uncomfortable.

She was almost as tall as Theo and willow-thin. Her dark hair was cut stylishly short and she looked striking in a pale green designer dress. But her appearance meant nothing; it was the information she had imparted. 'You can't stop now,' protested Dione.

'You two haven't known each other very long, have you?' enquired Theo's sister cautiously.

Dione shook her head, unwilling to tell her exactly how quickly this marriage had been arranged. She had gone through the ceremony as if in a dream and if anyone had asked her about it she wouldn't have been able to remember one thing. Not even declaring that she would be Theo's wife. All she had been aware of was him standing tall and strong at her side, and once, when she had faltered, he had caught her hand and squeezed it encouragingly.

Alexandra grinned now. 'Love at first sight? And they say it never happens. It's easy to see that you two are made for each other. He's been living in a world of his own since his divorce. It was never a happy marriage, kept together only for their son's sake. You're the best thing that's ever happened to him.'

Dione frowned and if possible her heartbeat quickened even more. 'Theo has a son?' she questioned breathlessly.

Alexandra shook her head. 'He died when he was only eleven months old. I don't think Theo's ever got over it. And Katina walked out on him afterwards. A swift divorce followed.'

'How awful for him,' said Dione reverently, seeing Theo in a new light. 'It's no wonder he can't bear to talk about it.' And she made up her mind there and then that she would never let on that she knew. Not unless he brought the subject up himself. And that was extremely unlikely under their surreal circumstances.

The day seemed endless. Theo dutifully stood at her side as a constant stream of his friends and relatives came to congratulate them and no one would have guessed that theirs was a marriage in name only. The way he looked at her, the way he touched her elbow, the way he smiled, made it all look very real. And Dione, too, smiled until her face ached, pretending a happiness she was far from feeling.

'You should have been an actor,' said Theo softly at

one point when she had just agreed that they were made for each other.

'You too,' she tossed back.

Phrosini dragged herself away from the hospital and came to add her further congratulations. 'Your father is very grateful for what you're doing,' she reassured Dione.

As well he should be Dione almost said, but she did not want to upset her stepmother so she smiled instead.

'Theo made a good choice with the dress.' It was slender and elegant and made Dione look even taller than she was.

'She is very beautiful,' agreed Theo, looking for all the world as though he was the proud groom. 'I think our marriage will be most agreeable. And definitely exciting.'

Dione wanted to ask him in what way, but not in front of Phrosini. All the arguments they would have perhaps? Definitely not exciting in a sexual sense. Of that she was very sure. And when Phrosini drifted away and for a few moments they were alone she asked him what he had meant.

'How will our marriage be exciting?'

'That's easy,' he said with a shrug of his wide shoulders. 'There will never be a dull moment with you, my sweet Dione. Sparks will fly, I'm very much aware of that, as I am aware of the fact that all day long you've wished yourself anywhere but at my side. You've stood the test admirably. Maybe it's time I added my congratulations?' And with that he bowed his head to kiss her.

Dione stiffened and moved so that his lips brushed her cheek, and she would have pushed him away had he not gripped her arm in warning. 'Careful, *agapi mou*, we're being watched.'

So Dione fixed the smile back on her face, hiding gritted teeth and a dislike so intense that it burnt into her soul. Thank goodness, she thought, that she hadn't agreed to his initial contract or she would have found herself in his bed tonight. In bed with a stranger! She shivered.

Immediately attentive, Theo asked, 'Are you cold?' And his liquid dark eyes were filled with concern.

Dione shook her head. 'Someone walking over my grave.' And, although it was a common expression, she felt that in this instance it was the truth. She might as well be dead as married to this obnoxious man.

No, that wasn't true. He wasn't obnoxious. He was virile and handsome and astonishingly wealthy, which made him attractive in most female eyes. It would have all been so much easier had she felt the same way. But being bought put a different perspective on things. She meant nothing more to Theo than a possession, nothing more than anything else he could have bought with his millions.

In fact she felt unclean and she would have liked nothing more than to run into the house and take a shower, and stay there for however long it took to make her feel whole and pure again. She had committed a sin in marrying Theo. She had made promises in the chapel that she knew she would not keep.

It was a relief when the day was over, when everyone had gone and she could relax her aching face.

'Well, Mrs Tsardikos,' said Theo with a satisfied smile, 'I've made many purchases in my life, but none as satisfactory as this.'

Dione frowned and her heart stammered fearfully. 'Satisfactory?' She didn't like the look on his face; it was as though he was contemplating pleasures to come.

If he thought he could ignore their contract he was wrong, very wrong. She wouldn't be averse to walking out of here right this very minute.

'I mean that you're the most beautiful wife any man could wish for. Congratulations have flown thick and fast.'

'And exactly what do you mean by wife?' asked Dione, appalled to hear how shrill her voice sounded.

'Just that. A beautiful, gracious lady. Someone I shall be pleased to show off.'

'And that's all?'

'What else could there be?' A well-shaped brow lifted enquiringly. 'Unless of course you're having second thoughts and are willing to share my bed?' Dark eyes captured hers so that it was difficult to look away.

Dione's heart drummed even faster. 'Not in a million years.'

Theo smiled in a way that told her he was confident that one day she would change her mind.

'I mean it!'

'Then why do you look so scared?' he asked. 'You can lock your door if you like. I'm a man of my word, Dione, in case you didn't know. As I said once before, the first move will come from you.'

Dione felt her body relax and she managed her first genuine smile of the day. 'You're a very honourable man, Theo, and I thank you for helping my father.'

'He doesn't have the money yet,' he pointed out.

Dione drew in a swift breath. 'I hope you're not going back on your word. I've completed my side of the bargain.'

'And it will be in his bank account first thing tomorrow morning.'

His steady eyes met hers but a faint feeling of unease returned. What if he was lying? What if he wanted to take her into his bed before paying her father? The sooner she went to her room and locked the door the better. She faked a yawn. 'I'm tired, Theo. I'd like to go to bed.'

'Running away?' he mocked.

Dione stood her ground, lifting her chin and looking right into those dark, dangerous eyes. 'Not at all. It's been a long day.' And she cursed herself when she felt something approaching a flutter in the pit of her stomach. She put it down to nerves. It couldn't possibly be anything else—could it?

'I'll walk you up. Maybe I'll retire myself. As you say, it's been a tiring day. But a satisfying one all the same, don't you agree?'

'Where my father's concerned, yes,' she snapped. 'For myself, no. The next twelve months are going to be sheer hell.'

A harsh shadow darkened his face as they mounted the stairs together. 'And you'd do that for your father— put yourself through hell?'

Dione nodded, not trusting herself to speak. Put like that, it seemed like an enormous unselfish gesture on her part. If Yannis hadn't been at death's door she wouldn't have done it; that was a fact. If Phrosini hadn't persuaded her… Tears began to sting the back of her eyes and she turned away. 'Goodnight, Theo.'

'Goodnight, my beautiful bride,' he answered as they reached her door. 'May I be permitted one kiss? To seal the deal perhaps?'

Dione wanted to say no, she wanted no contact between them, but she knew it would be churlish to refuse. It was going to be a brief kiss, though; nothing prolonged or sexual. Just a touching of lips.

She put her hand on his chest, prepared to push him away should he attempt to get too close, and felt passionate heat beneath her palm and the thud of his heart and knew immediately that she was in danger.

But it was too late to back away.

As his head swooped down narrowed lids hid the expression in his eyes, but his finger beneath her chin felt like a branding iron. This wasn't going the way she wanted.

Surprisingly, though, the kiss itself was restrained. His lips touched hers and then pulled swiftly away.

He was a man of honour after all.

Swift relief flooded through Dione's body and she felt herself go limp and would have fallen to the floor had Theo not caught her. His arms were strong and safe as he kicked open her door and carried her into the room, laying her gently on the bed.

'Thank you,' she whispered. 'I don't know what came over me.'

'The events of the day,' he tossed curtly. 'Will you be all right? Shall I send someone to help—'

'No!' cut in Dione swiftly. 'I'm fine now. I'd really like to be left alone.'

He nodded, his lips grim, and spun on his heel. Dione's relief knew no bounds when he finally shut the door behind him. She didn't even stop to question his sudden abruptness. This had been the worst possible day of her life and all she wanted to do was go to sleep and forget it.

Theo stalked into his room and tore off his clothes, leaving them untidily on the floor, before climbing beneath a fierce cold shower. Damn Dione! Damn the whole Keristari family! They were putting him through hell.

The money didn't count; it was a drop in the ocean to him, but Dione—she was a different proposition altogether. He had signed the wretched contract, he had promised to keep his hands off her. How the hell could he do that?

One touch was all it had taken to make him realise that he wanted her so badly that it would kill him to leave her alone. She was temptation incarnate. He could not imagine the days ahead without touching her, without kissing her, without making love to her. It would be sheer hell.

Maybe he should get out of here and leave her to her own devices? Maybe he should go on a world tour and forget her? Maybe he should just storm into her room and take her! This last thought fired the heat in his belly until it was at boiling point.

Damn! And damn again! What had he done?

It was a long time before Theo stepped out of the shower, feeling no better than he had before. This was a nightmare, a nightmare from which there was no escape—at least not for twelve long months. And maybe not even then. She would have got under his skin even more deeply.

With a towel wrapped around his loins he paced his room. Up and down he went like a caged lion. Up and down, round the bed and back again, until finally he went out onto the balcony and sat and watched the ocean. The restless ocean, a bit like himself with its endless to-ing and fro-ing.

He closed his eyes but all he could see was Dione's

beautiful face, and the thought that she would never be his pierced his heart like an arrow. He had intended to play the game slowly, to make her fall for him gradually without her knowing it—but how the hell could he do that when his body was on fire at the very thought of her lying in bed in the room next to him? When all he wanted to do was go in there and make love to her all night long?

It was what newly married couples usually did.

What a mistake it had been to believe that he could play these sorts of games. With other women, yes, perhaps. But not with Dione Keristari. He had fallen for her hook, line and sinker the first instant he saw her, despite how desperate she had looked. He admired her courage and her loyalty; she was a stronger person than he would ever be.

He got up and paced the balcony. It ran right around the house and all the upstairs rooms opened onto it. He came to a halt when he rounded the corner and saw Dione leaning against the rail, watching the ocean as he had done only seconds earlier. As soon as she saw him she turned to go back into her room but he held out his hand. 'Please, don't go.' And when she reluctantly halted he moved slowly towards her.

She had changed out of the wedding dress he had chosen with such care—how beautiful she had looked in it—and now wore a cream satin nightdress that barely covered either her breasts or her bottom. It had clearly been designed to tempt even the hardiest of men, and he wondered why she had chosen to wear it tonight of all nights.

Then suddenly she picked up a wrap and held it

tightly and defensively around her, as though she'd just realised that she was almost nude. It was a hot night, though, and he couldn't blame her for not wanting to wear much. He never wore anything in bed himself, and he was conscious now that all he had on was the towel. Perhaps she was thinking that his intentions were completely dishonourable.

'I couldn't sleep,' he said, by way of an apology.

'Me neither,' she admitted.

'I thought the sound of the ocean might lull you to sleep.'

'Well, it didn't. There's too much on my mind.'

'The same here.'

Lord, what a banal conversation to have with one's wife of a few hours, but what else could he say? He had promised to keep at arm's length but she was driving him crazy. That tempting glimpse of her body had sent his testosterone levels rising higher than they had ever been in his life. What was a man to do?

'Let's sit and watch the ocean together,' he said, in as normal a voice as he could muster. 'Would you like a drink, perhaps?'

'No, thanks, but yes, I will sit with you.'

Was that pain he heard in her voice? Was she doing it simply because she hadn't the strength to fight him? He sincerely hoped not. He didn't want her to hate him, even though he had more or less forced her into marriage.

It had been the only thing he could think of at the time so as not to let her slip away. The thought of never seeing her again had been abhorrent to him. It had been a foolish suggestion, he realised that now, and he could only hope that time would temper her resentment of him.

The moon was almost full and it lit the water like a fluorescent light, so that even without any lamps on in the house Theo could see Dione's face clearly. She looked sad and ethereal and it was the hardest thing in the world to keep his hands off her.

'How is Yannis?' he asked.

'I don't know.'

'He looked very frail at the wedding.'

'He is. Phrosini's very worried.'

'And you, are you worried?'

'Naturally,' she answered after a slight pause. 'I love my father. Why else would I have got myself into this situation?'

He wanted to say that Keristari didn't deserve her love, but he also wanted these few minutes together to be a time of peace not dissension and so he held his tongue. 'Do you think the money will help his health?' Privately, after having seen him today, Theo wasn't sure. He had looked at death's door.

'It's a lack of it that caused it,' she told him ruefully, 'so maybe it will. All we can do is pray and hope.'

'You're a good daughter to him.'

Dione didn't answer. She appeared deep in her own thoughts and they sat side-by-side in basket chairs and reflected over the turn of events that had brought them together.

Very soon he noticed that she had fallen asleep and gently he gathered her into his arms and carried her to her bed, where he laid her down and covered her with a single sheet. She did not wake and he stood there for a long time looking at this beautiful, untouchable lady.

So heavy was his heart when he finally went back to

his own room that he did not sleep. He spent the whole night thinking about Dione and wondering if it really would be possible to make her change her mind.

When Dione awoke her first thoughts were that she didn't remember getting into bed. She could remember sitting out on the balcony and Theo joining her, but nothing after that. Her body ran first hot and then cold at the thought that he might have put her to bed. And if he had, what else had he done? Had he looked at her? Touched her? Her robe had gone; she wore nothing but her ridiculous, minuscule nightdress. What had possessed her to wear it last night of all nights? What impression had she given?

Bouncing up, she took a cooling shower before dressing in a loose-fitting cotton top and a pair of cut-off jeans. She wanted nothing to give Theo the wrong impression.

But she had wasted her time. When she went downstairs he was nowhere in sight, and his housekeeper told her that he had gone to the office. 'He said to tell you that he is deeply sorry, this being the first day of your marriage, but something important came up. He says he will make it up to you tonight.' There was a twinkle in the buxom woman's eyes as she spoke, but to Dione it was a death sentence. Besides, Anna surely knew that they were sleeping in separate rooms?

'Thank you,' she said quietly.

Dione spent her day swimming and sunbathing and visiting her father. He didn't look any better and worried when the money was going to reach his account.

'I've kept my side of the bargain,' she assured him.

'Theo's gone to the office today; I expect he's arranging it.'

'He'd better be,' grumbled Yannis.

He didn't seem interested in the fact that she'd virtually sold her soul; all he wanted was the money. Dione hated him for it and didn't stay very long. And when she got home Theo was there.

'Where have you been?' he asked with a scowl dark enough to turn day into night.

'To see my father,' she answered haughtily. 'Is it any business of yours what I do with my time?'

'I thought you'd left.'

'Why would I do that?' she asked.

'You weren't happy last night.'

'I'm not happy today either, but that doesn't mean I won't keep my side of the bargain,' she retorted heatedly. 'Have you finalised things?'

Theo inclined his head. 'So now we can go away on honeymoon. I thought England. I thought you'd like to introduce me to your mother. Have you told her yet that she has a son-in-law?'

CHAPTER FIVE

As THEO'S plane touched down in England Dione felt her heart sinking even lower. The thought of telling her mother that she had secretly got married was bad enough. But there was Chris as well. How was she going to explain it to him?

Theo had done his best to engage her in conversation during the flight, but all Dione had wanted to do was shut herself away in her own miserable world and pretend he didn't exist. In the end he had lost his temper with her.

'If you don't make some sort of effort, Dione, everyone will know that our marriage is a sham. And I'm warning you, if it ever leaks out, your father will find himself in more trouble than ever before. A contract is a contract. You'd best remember that.'

His dark eyes, almost jet-black, had bored into her skull like surgeons' drills, and Dione's whole body had frozen. There was no disputing that this man meant what he said.

'I shall do nothing to back out of it,' she riposted, her head held high, her eyes as dark and threatening as his. 'You need have no fear of that.'

'Then why the distance?' he demanded, shoving his

face up close to hers. 'Why a journey as silent as the grave? Don't you think this is as bad for me as it is for you?'

Her eyes shot wide. And although he smelled gorgeous, although his sexuality was undisputed, she glared fiercely. 'Go to hell, Theo. You're enjoying this. Power is your life-stream. It's your succour; it's your everything.'

'Power in a business sense, yes,' he agreed, 'but in my private life it's very different. I don't want you to feel that you have to put a face on to the world; I want you to enjoy being married to me. I want you to relax and have fun, and I want to enjoy it too. We could do that, Dione, if you'd not look on me as some sort of monster.'

Dione almost laughed, for that was exactly how she did see him. A great big predatory monster, taking but never giving. He'd taken her in payment for helping out Yannis, and she didn't think she'd be far wrong in thinking that at some stage in their relationship he'd demand his pound of flesh. Promises were made to be broken and Theo Tsardikos wouldn't lose a second's sleep over it.

'In front of anyone who matters I'll be the perfect wife,' she assured him coolly, 'but when we're on our own…' She let her voice tail off, telling him without words that he'd best not expect anything that wasn't in their contract.

Theo's nostrils had flared as he turned to look out of the window, and now that they had touched down, his hand on her arm as he helped her alight was like a grip of iron.

A car met them and whisked them to a penthouse apartment on London's South Bank and all the time neither of them spoke. The views across the city from the floor-to-ceiling windows were amazing but Dione was in no mood to admire. Nor did she comment about the tasteful décor, or the fact that her room and Theo's had an adjoining door. She silently noted that there was a key in the lock, which she intended keeping firmly turned.

'So when am I going to meet your mother?' he asked, when they had showered and changed. 'Maybe we should invite her out for dinner if you think that would be easier. She won't be able to have hysterics in a crowded place.'

He had changed into black chinos and polo shirt open at the neck to reveal dark whorls of hair on his broad chest. Dione didn't particularly like men with hairy chests, but she had to admit that seeing Theo like this made her want to touch, to find out whether the hairs were softly smooth, or strong and springy. And he was wearing a different aftershave too, something less exotic but fresh and exciting, and which sent a surprising tingle through her nerve-ends.

'My mother will never have hysterics,' she informed him tersely, hating herself for feeling anything other than dislike. 'She'll be surprised, shocked even, but she'll accept the news quietly, like she does everything else in her life.'

Theo settled deeper into his chair, legs outstretched, ankles crossed. 'It doesn't sound as though she was much of a match for Yannis Keristari.'

Dione shrugged. 'I guess not.'

'So tell me about her. Tell me why their marriage didn't work out.'

But Dione shook her head. 'I'd rather not talk about it.' She wasn't ready to discuss such matters with Theo.

In reality he was her mother's son-in-law and should be told, but in her mind he was still an outsider, an outsider who had no time for her father, and he didn't merit such intimate details. She doubted she ever would tell him.

'It sometimes helps,' he said, with an understanding that surprised her. She hadn't realised that she was giving away her inner torment, though why it should still hurt after all these years she didn't know. Perhaps it always would. It was a popular belief that time healed but this particular wound seemed as though it would never go away.

Dione pushed herself up from the chair and walked across to the window, her back to Theo. 'Not on this occasion! In any case, considering our marriage isn't a normal one, I don't see that it's any of your business.'

'I'd like to make it mine.' He had risen silently and moved with surprising quietness for such a big man, and his gruff voice in her ear made her jump.

She swiftly turned and found herself chest-to-chest with him, only a hair's breadth separating them. The heat of his body reached out to her like an unseen hand and although she wanted to move she didn't want to give him the satisfaction of knowing that he disturbed her.

So she stood stock-still and looked into the amazing darkness of his eyes. Reflected in them was the blueness of the sky and the greyness of the buildings, making them a mixture of all three colours. They were shiny like glass and held her in their thrall for several long seconds.

Unaware that she had been holding her breath, Dione let it out on a sigh. 'Not now, Theo,' she said quietly, unsure whether she was saying not now to something more than his request. Something much more dangerous. For that was how it felt. Every one of her nerve-ends was vibrating as he continued to look at her with such deep meaning in his eyes that she knew she ought to move, and move quickly. Why was it, then, that her feet felt as though they were glued to the floor?

In the end it was Theo who turned away, but not before a satisfied smile curved his generous lips. 'If you can't make a decision then I'll make it for you,' he said. 'We'll go and see your mother, tell her our news, and then if she hasn't eaten we'll take her out for a meal.'

'What if she's not in?' she asked, wanting to put off the moment for as long as she could, but thankful that Theo had moved because she could now draw in a deep breath without feeling that she was being consumed by him.

'We'll cross that bridge when we come to it. Something tells me that you're not looking forward to telling her that we're married. It will be a shock, I know, and she'll be disappointed that she wasn't invited, but leave it to me—I'll win her over.'

And Dione didn't doubt that he would.

Theo Tsardikos was a charmer of the highest order. Already, after only one day of a marriage she hadn't wanted, she was beginning to feel a faint physical attraction. It could never be anything else. She hated him for trapping her the way he had, but she had to admit he was the sexiest male she had met in a very long time. Chris was nothing compared to Theo.

Perhaps she ought to tell Theo about Chris now, before her mother dropped it out? But he was already ushering her towards the door and the moment passed.

Dione had a key to her mother's house but today she did not let herself in. She rang the bell and waited, conscious of Theo standing, tall and authoritative, behind her shoulder. She had to ring a second time before the door was opened and she'd been hoping that she had a reprieve.

'Darling,' said Jeannie, her pale blue eyes lighting up as she gave her daughter a hug. 'What a wonderful surprise! I thought you were still in Greece.' And then she saw Theo and there was an unspoken question in her frown. 'Do come in.'

They followed her mother into her small, cluttered, but comfortable sitting room and Dione was conscious of Theo filling it with his presence. He was such a big man and her mother was small and quite frail, with brown hair already beginning to go grey.

'How's Yannis?' asked Jeannie, though it was clear that she was still wondering who her daughter's companion was.

'Not good,' answered Dione, glad of a reprise from the moment of introduction. She had no idea how her mother would take it. At this moment Jeannie couldn't take her eyes off Theo. And who could blame her? He was terribly handsome and simply oozed charm. Even though so far he hadn't spoken a word his smile had said everything.

'I'm sorry to hear that,' answered her mother. 'And is this—a friend of your father's?'

'Mmm, actually, no. Well, yes, I suppose in a way; he's a business acquaintance,' muttered Dione, feeling her face flood with colour.

'I see.'

Dione knew that she didn't, and the more she fought for the right words the hotter she became. This was going to be far worse than she had imagined. And unconsciously she began fiddling with the rings on her finger, the huge solitaire diamond and the exquisite gold band.

Jeannie let out a scream. 'Dione, you're married!'

Theo came to her rescue. 'And I'm the lucky man. How nice it is meet you, Mrs Keristari.'

Silence filled the room, the sonorous ticking of an old grandfather clock the only sound.

How much time passed Dione didn't know, but it felt like hours. Her mother's face was filled with both surprise and dismay. Not a woman to give vent to her feelings, she let her eyes do the talking. And she didn't look happy.

Theo was the first to speak. 'I'm Theodossus Tsardikos, usually called Theo.' And he held out his hand.

Jeannie was a long time in taking it, and even then she didn't speak; her blue eyes were clouded and distrusting.

'I'm sorry our marriage has come as such a shock to you, Mrs Keristari,' he said, smiling warmly and reassuringly. 'It did happen rather suddenly, I admit. But when love strikes, why wait?' And he put his arm about Dione's shoulders and kissed her full on the lips.

A shiver ran through her, trickling down her spine like melting ice. Although the kiss had meant nothing it set off a chain reaction that was completely unexpected. Something she would have to analyse later. She didn't know whether to curse Theo or thank him. She hadn't completely made up her mind whether to tell her mother the truth, or stick to the lie that she and Theo were happily married. He had taken that option away from her.

Jeannie certainly wouldn't approve of her marrying Theo to help out her father. Not after the way he had treated them both. So perhaps it was as well that her mother didn't know the truth. Not at this stage anyway. Maybe some time in the future when it was all over. When she and Theo were divorced and she could get on with her life.

Jeannie's eyes were on Dione now, asking her how it had happened.

'I'm sorry, Mum,' she said quietly, her lovely dark eyes sad and caring. 'I know it's come as a shock, but it really did happen like Theo says. Lightning struck us. We knew we had to be together.'

'You could have told me,' whispered the older woman.

'I know, but there wasn't even time to fly you over to Greece for the wedding. I didn't think you'd come anyway because of—'

'Yes, I understand,' said Jeannie, though it was clear that she didn't see the reason for such urgency. Then she added politely, 'Welcome into the family, Theo.'

'I apologise for keeping you in ignorance,' he said, taking her hand and kissing the back of it in an exaggerated gesture. 'We only married the day before yesterday—it was a complete whirlwind affair—and we made it our first priority to come over here and tell you. Your daughter is wonderful and I know that we're going to be very happy.'

Goodness, don't lay it on with a trowel, thought Dione, though she dutifully smiled into Theo's face. 'We are,' she agreed.

And after a few more consoling sentences from Theo Jeannie finally relaxed and smiled and wished them all the best.

Hurdle number one over, thought Dione as they sat drinking tea a few minutes later. Theo already had her mother eating out of the palm of his hand, even blushing when he complimented her on looking too young to have a daughter of marriageable age.

'Does Theo know about Chris?' asked her mother, when Theo excused himself with a business call some time later.

Dione shook her head and looked guilty.

'Why not?'

'I saw no point.'

'And Chris himself, I know he isn't aware of your marriage because I saw him only yesterday. What are you going to say to him? Really, Dione, this is very unlike you. You always swore you would never get married to a Greek because of what happened with your father.'

Dione could understand her mother's concern where Chris was concerned. She was worried herself about how she was going to tell him. Maybe she could persuade her mother to do it for her? No, that wouldn't be fair; it was the coward's way out. She would have to go and see him and hope he wouldn't be too angry.

'Theo's different from my father,' she said defensively. 'He'll never hurt me the way Father hurt you.'

Jeannie pursed her lips. 'I hope you're right.'

'Mrs Keristari.' Theo came back into the room. 'I'd very much like to spend more time getting to know you. Let us take you out to dinner. We'll have your favourite wine and your favourite food and—'

'Please, call me Jeannie,' she said, interrupting him. 'And thank you for the offer but I've eaten. I was about to settle down and watch my favourite TV programme.'

'Then we are interrupting you. I'm so sorry. How about tomorrow night?'

'Tomorrow I'm…'

When her mother hesitated Dione knew that she was trying to make excuses. She didn't want to dine with Theo. Her mother wasn't used to such flattery, such attention—she found it embarrassing. And when the doorbell rang Jeannie fled to answer it.

'Don't push my mother,' warned Dione quietly. 'You're overwhelming her. She leads a very simple life.'

'So I'm beginning to realise. You're really nothing like her, are you? You're the feistiest woman I've ever met. I guess you take after your father in that respect.'

'I just know how to stick up for myself,' answered Dione. 'My mother doesn't. But nevertheless she's the sweetest woman alive. I've hated lying to her about us.'

'I thought she took it remarkably well, after her initial shock. And I—'

'Dione! You're home!'

Her words were cut off by an all too familiar voice, and a pair of strong arms lifted her off the floor and swung her around. Dione caught sight of her mother shaking her head, informing her that she hadn't told Chris about Theo. She looked terrified. Jeannie hated altercations, would do anything to avoid them, and now she was going to be stuck in the middle of one.

And of course Theo didn't know about Chris either.

CHAPTER SIX

WHEN Chris put her down and tried to kiss her Dione pushed her hands against his chest. Goodness, this was a worst-case scenario. She had no idea that Chris visited her mother. She had been hoping to go and see him alone, break the news without Theo breathing over her shoulder.

Chris was much shorter than Theo with sandy-coloured hair and a pale complexion. For several months she had thought she was in love with him , and had been truly upset when she'd heard that he was seeing his ex-girlfriend again. In fact when she went to Greece she had taken her ring off. For one reason she hadn't wanted her father to know, and for another she'd begun to have second thoughts about marrying him. If he could go out with a former girlfriend before they were married, what would he do afterwards?

Perhaps it was one of the reasons she'd agreed to marry Theo? Surely she wouldn't have done so if she'd been really, truly and deeply in love with Chris? If she'd trusted him with her heart and soul?

Finally Chris noticed that there was someone else in

the room. A tall, dark, Hellenic-looking man with a harsh frown on his handsome face.

Dione hesitated for only a fraction of a second, knowing the disclosure was going to hurt him, but she had to get it over with and the sooner the better. 'Chris, this is Theo, my—my husband.'

'Husband? You're married?' Chris' voice rose to ear-splitting proportions and his faced flushed an ugly red. 'What the hell's going on? You're supposed to be engaged to me.'

Dione heard Theo draw in a harsh breath and knew that she dared not look at him. 'I—I was going to tell you, Chris, but it all happened so quickly. Theo swept me off my feet. He proposed, I accepted, and two days later we were married. I'm so sorry.'

'I bet you're sorry,' Chris sneered. 'Some jerk with loads of money turned your head.' He flashed a disparaging look in Theo's direction. 'And don't bother to deny it, big guy, because I've met your sort before. I saw the limo outside, wondered whose it was. Quite a catch, aren't you?'

'I don't think you entirely understand,' said Theo, his voice very even, though Dione could see fire in his eyes.

'Then make me,' tossed Chris, his blue eyes hard and belligerent.

Dione had never seen this side of Chris. Initially she had felt sorry for him but now he was behaving like a maniac and she was afraid.

'The way I see it,' retorted Theo, his voice crackling with tightly controlled anger, 'Dione couldn't have been truly in love with you or she wouldn't have given me a second glance.'

'Oh, you think that, do you?' scoffed Chris. 'It proves how little you know. It's easy to see that you turned her head by flashing your wallet.'

'And you think money is important, do you?' demanded Theo. 'You think Dione would throw away the love of her life, if that's what you believe you are, for the security of knowing that she need never work again? I think, my friend, that you do not know Dione very well at all.'

Dione glared at them both and put her hand on Chris' arm. 'Please stop it!'

'Why should I,' raged Chris, 'when you drop me for some scheming bastard?' He shook her away and stood in front of Theo. 'I ought to knock the living daylights out of you.'

'Feel free,' answered the handsome Greek, arms folded across his magnificent chest.

Chris was the first to back down, though his eyes were still murderous.

'I think we should go,' whispered Dione to Theo.

'Not until he's left,' he answered calmly. 'I don't want him upsetting your mother any further.'

Chris looked at Jeannie, as though imploring her to let him stay, but Dione's mother nodded. 'I think it might be best.' She looked tortured at the scene that had just taken place.

When Chris had left, banging the door loudly behind him, Dione took her mother's hand. 'I'm truly sorry. I never expected Chris to behave like that. He's not the man I thought he was. Does he visit you often?'

Jeannie shrugged. 'A couple of times a week; sometimes more. He comes for his dinner and we sit and chat and—'

'He's taking advantage of you, Mother,' insisted Dione. 'You know he hates cooking for himself. You must stop it.'

'I don't expect he'll come again now that he knows you're—married.' She said the word with difficulty and Dione hugged her.

'I'm sorry, Mother.'

'It's all right. Didn't you say something about going for a meal? Isn't it time you went?'

'You mean you want to be alone?'

Jeannie nodded.

'Then we'll go,' said Dione.

It was Theo's turn to voice his concern. 'Are you sure you'll be all right, Jeannie?'

Again Jeannie nodded. 'I'm sorry Chris spoke to you the way he did.'

'No need to apologise,' he said at once. 'I guess I wouldn't have been happy if the positions were reversed.'

Indeed, thought Dione. He would have been spitting mad; the other guy might not have got off quite so lightly.

Outside in the car there was a terrible silence and she realised that Theo hadn't started the engine. Instead he sat there looking at her, anger on his face, and his voice was dangerously cool when he spoke. 'Why didn't you tell me about your fiancé?'

'Would it have made a difference?' she demanded to know. 'Would you have given my father the money without any conditions? I don't think so.'

'So you selflessly gave up your boyfriend?' His dark eyes were savage on hers. 'Or perhaps it wasn't so selfless. How the hell could you have got yourself engaged to an unscrupulous swine like him? He's treating your mother abominably. He's using her, he's sponging off her.'

'I know,' said Dione quietly. 'And I'm appalled. He used to come round for his dinner quite often when I was there, but I never imagined that he'd carry on doing it.'

'Your mother's too kind.'

Dione nodded. How very true that was.

'It looks to me as though I've saved you from a fate worse than death. How the worm turns, isn't that what they say?'

Dione said nothing. She was too busy wondering about the change in Chris.

Theo's lips tightened and he turned the key. The car roared into life and sped down the road. But they didn't go out to dinner; they went back to his apartment instead.

Once inside, a glass of whisky in his hand, he resumed the conversation. 'How much does this man mean to you?' Dark eyes were hard and questioning and his whole body was taut with suppressed anger.

Dione shrugged, trying to appear uninterested, whereas deep inside she was a mass of unhappy nerves. 'Does it really matter?' Actually Chris meant nothing now. He had well and truly blotted his copybook as far as she was concerned. Never for one minute had she expected him to behave so bullishly. And to take advantage of her mother—that was the last straw.

Theo snorted. 'I can't see you giving up a man you truly love to help your father. No girl would do that. Especially for a bully like Keristari! Or is that it? He bullied you into it. Threatened to make your life hell if you didn't help him out?'

'Nothing of the sort,' declared Dione with a toss of

her head, eyes flashing pure resentment. 'The choice was purely mine.'

Dark brows rose. 'And I'm expected to believe that? I did do, until I found out about your fiancé. He had every right to be angry. I'd have killed if the positions were reversed.'

'Just before I left England I found out that he'd been seeing his ex-girlfriend,' said Dione quietly.

'Ah!' Enlightenment filled Theo's eyes. 'So you'd have ended the engagement anyway?'

'I guess so,' she acknowledged, not wanting to keep up the tension any longer. She felt drained of all energy. It had been a long day. All she wanted to do was go to bed; she wasn't even hungry.

'Perhaps I did you a favour?' His lips curled in amusement and his body relaxed. 'Care to join me in a drink before dinner?'

Dione shook her head. 'I want neither. I'm tired.' But she was glad that the topic was over, that he'd accepted her engagement would have ended anyway. Not that she could see him caring even if she'd been truly and deeply in love with Chris. He was playing a game with her and her father, and enjoying it. It wouldn't matter to him one jot if he hurt anyone's feelings.

She turned and headed for the door but Theo was quicker. A heavy hand dropped on her shoulder and spun her round to face him. 'You're not turning in yet. You're my wife, Dione, and I want your company. Indeed, I demand it.'

After the last few days when she'd gone around in a trance, not really believing all that was happening to her, this was the last straw as far as Dione was concerned. 'You demand it?' she flashed. 'Well, tough luck, because I'm going! There's nothing in our contract to say that I have to play the part of a loving wife when there's no one else around. Or had you forgotten that?'

Theo didn't seem in the least perturbed by her outburst. In fact, he smiled and shook his head. 'Have you any idea how tempting you look when your eyes are flashing fire and your whole body is alive?' His normally faint accent had deepened, as had his voice, and his meaning was very clear.

Theo was disappointed when Dione backed away. He didn't want her to be afraid of him; it wasn't in his plan of things at all. She was totally, gorgeously sexy, and every part of him strained to touch and to kiss and finally to take her into his bed.

Although he had agreed to her ridiculous contract he had no intention of biding by it. He was a red-blooded male not used to keeping his hands off his women friends.

And this was not just a friend, she was his wife!

This was their honeymoon!

Her place was in his bed!

He would allow her some freedom but his patience wouldn't last long. Even now his male hormones were running riot. And when Dione moved away he had to bite back a savage response.

'Don't be afraid, my beautiful wife. I have no intention of going back on my word, but there's nothing to stop me complimenting you! You're every man's dream, do you know that?'

'No, I don't,' she snapped. 'And compliments like that will get you nowhere.'

'I don't expect they will,' he answered evenly. She was an amazing girl, nothing at all like her mother, who was gentle and quietly spoken. What Jeannie had ever seen in Yannis Keristari he didn't know. They were poles apart. Maybe Keristari had thought he could mould her into his way of thinking. Obviously the woman had a backbone of steel; otherwise she would never have been able to back out of their marriage. Good for her, he thought.

He liked Jeannie; he liked her very much. But he had taken an instant dislike to Chris Donovan. What a swine the man was. What a manipulative swine. He couldn't understand what Dione had ever seen in him. She could certainly have done better. If at the end of these twelve months they went their separate ways then he hoped she would find someone who truly loved her and whom she loved in return.

She deserved that at least.

'I'd like you to have dinner with me,' he said, not wanting her to go to her room yet. Not at all, if he could help it. He wanted her to share his bed, tonight and every night. It was going to be sheer hell keeping his hands off her. 'My housekeeper's an angel; she'll be able to rustle something up in no time at all.'

'I'm not hungry,' she insisted.

With difficulty he held back his anger. 'You've had nothing since breakfast, Dione. You won't be able to sleep on an empty stomach.'

'That will be my problem, not yours,' she retorted.

Harshness crept into his voice. 'You're my wife; I want to look after you. I insist that you eat.'

Dione glared at him, her eyes brilliant with anger, and he wanted to take her into his arms and tell her that everything would be all right. But would it? She had married him for one reason only. A ridiculous reason, as far as he was concerned. Keristari didn't deserve her loyalty, and he wouldn't be averse to telling him so if the opportunity ever presented itself.

'It looks like you're giving me no choice,' she said, her head tilted high, her eyes bright with indignation and anger.

Lord, she looked beautiful. His hormones surged once again and he had to move away or he would have taken her into his arms and kissed her.

When he gave his ultimatum he hadn't realised quite how irresistible she would be and he took a few deep breaths as he went to find his housekeeper.

Left alone, Dione breathed in deeply as well. She was fully aware that Theo found her attractive and she wished that she had been strong enough to stick to her guns and go to her room. On the other hand, it could be fun taunting him but remaining cool and unobtainable at the same time. It was no less than he deserved.

When he returned she was sitting in one of the easy chairs, her legs crossed, revealing a tantalising amount of thigh. If he saw he ignored it, crossing to the corner bar and pouring himself another Scotch. 'What can I get you?' he asked after he'd taken a long swallow. 'A gin and tonic? Martini? Wine?'

He knew so little about her that he had no idea she never drank. 'Just a tonic water, thank you, with ice and lemon.'

'Nothing stronger?'

'I don't touch alcohol.'

Brows rose. 'Any particular reason?'

'I saw my father drink enough,' she answered tersely.

'Ah! I wondered why you didn't touch your champagne at the wedding.'

Dione hadn't realised that he'd noticed. She'd made a pretence of drinking, raising her glass to her lips whenever the occasion demanded it.

'Would you rather I didn't drink?' he asked.

'Of course not,' she said at once.

He handed her the crystal glass and sat down opposite, studiously ignoring her legs, letting his glittering eyes rest on her face instead.

So he could be a gentleman!

And yet Dione didn't think that his thoughts were quite so gentlemanly. She wasn't an idiot; she knew that he wanted her, and that this whole marriage agreement was going to be harder than she thought. It would be up to her to be the strong one.

They sat talking about not very much until his housekeeper told them that dinner was ready. The table was set in a formal dining room and they had chicken consommé followed by cheese omelette and salad and then raspberry parfait. All very light and delicious and Dione surprised herself by eating every bit.

Afterwards they took their coffee back into the living area and moved out onto a wide, glass-enclosed balcony with sliding doors that could be opened or closed at will. It was enhanced with exotic palms and colourful plants, and they sat and watched the lights coming on over London. The sky turned dramatically pink and grey and finally into midnight blue, and for the first time Dione felt relaxed in Theo's company.

'I love your apartment,' she said impulsively.

'It does have its finer points,' he agreed.

'Do you spend much time here?'

'A couple of months a year, maybe, split up into the odd week or even a day, depending on my workload.'

'It seems a waste,' said Dione pensively. 'It's so lovely.'

'But not as lovely as you.'

Dione suddenly realised that he was watching her and not the beautiful vista in front of them, and heat filled her body. 'You don't have to flatter me,' she said smoothly, 'this isn't a proper marriage, you know.'

'If it were we wouldn't be sitting here now,' Theo returned. 'We'd be in bed, Dione. This is to all intents and purposes our honeymoon.' There was a moment's silence before he muttered, 'I never dreamt that I'd be spending it in this way.'

His face was in shadow, almost as dark as the night because there were no lights on in the room behind them, but both his words and his harsh voice told her that he wasn't happy at the prospect of sleeping alone.

'You knew what you were letting yourself in for,' she pointed out, even though her heart was drumming against her chest wall. There was no denying that Theo was an exciting male animal and remaining immune to him didn't look like a very good possibility.

Without any warning Theo pushed himself to his feet. 'I'm going to bed. Stay here if you like.' His voice was cold and abrupt and Dione guessed it was because she had reminded him of the terms of their contract.

'I think I will,' she said softly. At least until she felt sure that Theo was safely in his bed. Their rooms were far too close for comfort and she had no idea whether the adjoining door was locked or not. She ought to have checked it in front of him, when he was showing her around, made sure that he knew what the rules were.

'Goodnight, then,' he said tersely.

'Goodnight, Theo.'

He brushed past her and her skin tingled, and even when he had gone she could not relax. Exactly what had she let herself in for?

It must have been a good half-hour later before she finally went to bed, and by then Dione was so tired that she forgot to check the key in the lock.

CHAPTER SEVEN

'DON'T fight, you're coming with me!'

'No, Daddy, no! You're hurting!'

'Then do as I say, child!'

'I don't want to go with you; I want to stay with Mummy.' And she screamed as loud as she could.

Dione felt strong arms around her and struggled violently. 'Get away, *get away*!'

'Dione,' came the insistent voice, a different voice this time, 'wake up! Do you hear me? Wake up.'

Dione struggled to open her eyes, and instead of her father she saw Theo. A strong, protective, concerned Theo. And realised that it had all been a dream, the recurring nightmare that had haunted her over the years.

Tears rolled down her cheeks unchecked as she let Theo hold and comfort her. He found a handkerchief from somewhere and dabbed her cheeks, and she took it from him and held it to her eyes.

Several long minutes passed before her sobs subsided and her shoulders stopped heaving. 'I—I'm sorry,' she stammered.

'Don't be, *agapi mou*. Are you all right now?'

Dione nodded.

'Would you like anything? A glass of water perhaps? Or would you like me to keep holding you?'

'Yes, please,' she whispered, snuggling into his chest. Surprisingly she felt safe in Theo's arms; safe and cared for. And although she knew it was dangerous, although he wore nothing but a pair of black boxers, she wanted him to stay with her for the rest of the night.

He stroked her sweat-streaked hair back from her face and murmured words of comfort, and not until she had completely calmed down did he say, 'Do you want to tell me about it?'

Dione had never thought she would disclose to Theo what had happened to her as a child, but suddenly she wanted him to know. There could be other nights when she screamed and thrashed in her bed and woke him. She owed him the truth at least.

'It's about my father,' she said unevenly.

Theo drew in a swift breath and held her even more tightly. 'Go on,' he said, and she could hear a thread of anger in his voice.

'I was only six years old,' she confessed, 'and he thought my mother was having an affair with another man—not that I knew that at the time—and he turned out to be wrong anyway. But because of that he decided she wasn't fit to bring up his child and he dragged me from my bed in the middle of the night and bundled me in his car and flew me to Greece.'

She faltered a moment. This was the first time she had told anyone what had happened and it was a momentous occasion for her. 'He never returned here,' she finished with a break in her voice. 'He hasn't seen my mother since.'

Against her body Dione felt all of Theo's muscles tighten and a hiss of anger escape his lips. 'The swine! You must have been terrified.'

'I was,' she agreed huskily. 'I didn't stop crying for days and days, and when I could cry no more I was terribly naughty, the most evil child imaginable. I think there were times when he wished he'd left me with my mother. But then he had a letter from my mother's solicitor about her rights, and he used to let me go to see her, not without a bodyguard of course. He needed to make sure I'd return,' she added disparagingly.

Dione's heart had used to break every time she had to leave her mother, and Jeannie would hug her through their tears and tell her that it wouldn't be long before she saw her again. In later years Dione had grown to understand that her mother had been too scared to go against Yannis' wishes in case he stopped her from seeing her daughter altogether.

'And yet you stayed with him, even when you were old enough to do your own thing?' questioned Theo in a quiet, puzzled voice. 'I don't understand that.'

Dione drew in a deep breath and let it go slowly. 'Because I was afraid he might still do something to hurt my mother. She's always felt deeply vulnerable where my father's concerned. He hurt her so much that she's never really got over it.'

Theo's arms tightened around her, and his mouth dropped tiny, comforting kisses on her brow. 'Poor lady! For what it's worth, I like her. She's sweet and gentle and she hated to see me and Chris fighting over you. It's what held me back. What did you ever see in him?'

Dione shrugged, glad for a moment of a change of topic. She had felt as if she was baring her soul, and it was painful, even though Theo seemed to understand. 'Maybe I was looking for love. He seemed like the right guy at the time.'

'And now?'

'I think you know the answer to that.' Dione could feel herself growing more and more comfortable in Theo's arms. Perhaps a little too comfortable, because somewhere deep inside her stirred dangerous feelings.

'My parents eventually got divorced,' she said, trying to ignore what was happening to her, 'and Yannis married Phrosini. I grew to love her. She's very dear to me. And she's good for my father too.'

'He doesn't bully her like he does everyone else?' asked Theo tersely.

'Phrosini gives as good as she gets. She's a very strong woman.'

'She'd need to be,' muttered Theo. 'And it's made you strong too, though not strong enough to tell your father to go to hell when he asked you to come and see me. Not that I'm objecting to it,' he added, tapping her nose with a gentle finger. 'You're the best thing that's happened to me in a long time.'

'Even when I scream like a baby and wake you from your sleep?' she asked with a rueful smile.

'Even then,' he agreed and, gathering her even more closely against him, he added, 'You don't deserve any of this, Dione.'

'It happened a long time ago,' she said. 'I should be over it.'

'Childhood memories are difficult to erase, especially of something as traumatic as that. Maybe you need to see someone.'

'A therapist, you mean?'

'Perhaps.'

Dione shook her head. 'It's only under times of stress that my nightmare returns.'

'So being here with me is a strain for you?' His lips firmed, and she felt a slight shift in his body. But he didn't move away because he was enjoying holding her, enjoying the warmth of her body against his, and she was very well aware that his hormones had kicked in and were ready to bounce into action.

As were her own! But she ignored them. 'Of course it's a strain. Being driven into a loveless marriage would be a strain for anyone.' As if he didn't know! But to him it was a pleasant game, maybe even an exciting one. He had no current girlfriend—at least she didn't think so—so he could afford to take a year out of his life and play games with her.

'I don't want it to be a strain for you,' he said, his voice a low rumble of sexuality. 'I want you to relax and enjoy our time together. Twelve months will be an age if you fight me.'

'So long as you keep your side of the bargain, I won't fight,' she reminded him, trying to ignore the swiftness of her heartbeats when his fingertips brushed the soft skin of her cheek. They traced her high cheekbone and the contours of her eyes and then trailed down the length of her nose. And finally he cupped her chin and turned her face up to his.

His eyes were as dark as the night, with just a tiny highlight in the pupil from the lamp he had switched on. Ninety-nine per cent of her told her to move away swiftly. The other one per cent was held in his thrall.

The male scent of him assaulted her nostrils, filtering through her senses until she felt drugged. And when his mouth came down over hers Dione had neither the strength nor the will-power to turn away.

Theo also seemed to forget that kissing or even any form of contact was taboo—unless, of course, he'd taken her lack of resistance as acceptance. Dione didn't even begin to think about that possibility, not when his mouth began a fiery assault that wrestled a powerful response from her. It was the most drugging kiss she had ever experienced and a murmur of satisfaction escaped unchecked from her lips.

'*Theos!*' groaned Theo, and, taking the sound as a form of surrender, he deepened the kiss, his tongue now entering her mouth, exploring, entwining, tasting and taking.

Dione felt herself spiralling up to an hitherto unexplored plane, sensation following sensation, touching nerve-ends, racing through veins, until it reached the most private part of her body, where it tightened and throbbed and made her very much aware of her vulnerability.

Theo was a highly dangerous man; he would be an even more dangerous lover. If he could arouse her like this by one simple kiss, what could he do if he really tried?

And why wasn't she fighting him off?

She had no wish to participate in sex with Theo Tsardikos for the next twelve months—for sex was all it would be—and then dissolve their marriage as though it had never happened. If it was what *he* wanted, it certainly wasn't on her agenda.

And yet she was allowing the kiss, not wanting it to stop; wanting Theo to stay with her for the rest of the night in case she had her nightmare again. But expecting him to lie with her and not touch her would be asking the impossible, she knew that, and it would be best to banish him now.

How could she, though, when she was enjoying his kisses so much? So much that they frightened her! Even so, she found herself kissing him back, so desperately that shame should have hung over her. Instead she felt a strange exhilaration, something that had never happened before.

Maybe because she'd never kissed anyone like Theo before!

He was a man of stature, of means, of immense sex appeal, and he was surely irresistible to any girl he met. And shame on her, she had joined the list, the only difference being that she had a gold band on her finger.

A band that meant nothing, she reminded herself, even as she trailed her fingers through the dark, springy hair on his muscular chest. Soft they were, the hairs, soft and silky, and she had an urge to nuzzle her face into them and inhale his manly fragrance. Of course, she didn't. Instead she splayed her fingers and pushed him away.

A faint smile curved his beautifully sculpted lips. He didn't look disappointed, but neither did he look triumphant that he had achieved something that she had vowed would never happen.

'Feeling better?' he asked.

Dione nodded, not trusting herself to speak. She was so filled with emotion that her throat had closed up.

'A kiss soothes most wounds,' he said with a faint smile, his eyes dark and unreadable. 'At least, that's what my mother used to tell me.'

'Not quite the sort of kiss you just gave me,' she countered.

Theo shrugged. 'If it did the trick, who cares?'

I care, she thought, because you've opened my defences. 'I think I'll be all right now,' she told him, her voice low and faintly shaky. Not surprising considering that her insides still sizzled. Kissing Theo was the most alarming thing that had ever happened to her. An experience she did not wish to repeat.

A little voice inside her head told her that she was lying, that she would dearly love Theo to kiss her again, that in fact she would like him to spend the rest of the night with her. But she ignored it.

'Are you sure?'

Dione nodded, not trusting herself to speak again.

Theo eased himself reluctantly from the bed and stood looking down at her, his arms folded over his hard, wide chest. His skin gleamed gold in the lamp light; even his ebony hair had a sheen. He was a perfect specimen of manhood and yet Dione knew the danger of getting too deeply involved.

As if marrying him wasn't deep enough!

'I'll leave the door open,' he said now, 'and then if you should need me you only have to call.'

Dione smiled faintly. She wouldn't be calling out again. In fact, it was doubtful whether she'd sleep. His kisses had completely obliterated all other thoughts and emotions.

He bent low over her. 'Goodnight, then, Dione.' And he kissed her again, but this time it was the sort of gentle kiss one would give a child. Nevertheless it had an alarming effect on her and she closed her eyes tightly and held her breath, listening as he moved softly out of the room, only then releasing it on a low, deep sigh.

At first she lay awake thinking about what had happened, wondering what the repercussions would be; whether Theo would now expect more from her. If so he was going to be deeply disappointed. He had caught her at her most vulnerable but she would make sure that it never happened again.

And as she lay thinking sleep overtook her, a dreamless sleep this time, and she woke to feel the warm rays of the morning sun streaming over her through the half-open curtains.

'How are you feeling? No more bad dreams?'

Shock made her eyes shoot open and she sat bolt upright in bed. 'What the devil are you doing here?'

Dark brows rose. 'Now, there's a friendly greeting after what happened last night.'

'I appreciate you comforting me,' she answered, feeling uncomfortable with Theo in the room, 'but as for anything else, it's totally out of order.'

'It didn't seem like that a few hours ago,' he snorted.

'I didn't know what I was doing.' She doubted he'd believe the lie because even to her own ears it sounded feeble.

'So that's how you usually get comforted, is it?' he sneered.

Dione shook her head in disbelief. 'You have a sick mind. I wasn't thinking straight last night; I didn't know what I was doing. But now I do, and rest assured it will never happen again.'

A tight smile twisted his lips. 'Is that a promise?'

He looked as though he didn't believe her and that made her even angrier. She slid out of bed and stood facing him with her arms akimbo, heedless of the fact that she wore only a short cotton nightdress, made even shorter where her hands bunched it up on her hips.

'I thought you were a man of your word, Theo Tsardikos. Clearly I was wrong. You took advantage of me in my hour of need and for that I hate you.'

'I took advantage?' snorted Theo, raising disbelieving brows. 'I didn't notice you attempting to fight me. I remember very clearly saying that you'd have to make the first move, and in my eyes you did just that. Rubbing your body against me as you did was nothing short of an invitation. Hell, Dione, I'm not made out of stone.'

'I hate you!' she flared. 'Now, get out of here and let me get showered and dressed.' Thankfully Theo was already dressed so his magnificent body was covered. Not that she couldn't remember what he looked like almost naked! The sight of all that bare flesh would remain with her for a very long time to come.

There was a distinct atmosphere over breakfast and when he asked her what she would like to do afterwards she glared at him. 'I'd like to go and see my mother—alone.'

'I'm afraid not,' he announced grimly. 'This is our honeymoon.'

'Honeymoons are for lovers, not enemies,' she retorted, her voice edged with anger.

'Then we'll have to see about turning me from an enemy to a lover, won't we?' he growled.

And Dione could see that he meant it. There was grim determination on his face, and cold, hard sincerity in his eyes. 'You'll have your work cut out,' she tossed back. 'Every time I look at you I think of my father. I'm doing it for him, not for your personal gratification.'

'But imagine the fun you could have while your father's counting my money.'

'My father's very ill,' she spat. 'How dare you talk about him like that?'

Theo shrugged. 'Not so ill that he didn't think twice about using you! And since I've parted with a very large sum I intend getting my money's worth. Remember that, Dione, the next time you think about hitting back at me. We can do this the easy way or the hard way; the choice is yours.'

CHAPTER EIGHT

THEO knew that he shouldn't have got annoyed with Dione, but it was hard trying to keep his hands off her. He had seen his opportunity last night and taken it and he didn't have any regrets.

Kissing her had been even better than he'd imagined. In his mind he'd not only kissed her but also made love to her; long, passionate sessions when the world had spun on its axis and he had gloried in the deal that he'd made.

And last night, after he'd gone back to his room, his body in torment, he'd hoped that it was the beginning of something special and exciting. Dione was a league apart from other girls. Usually they were out for what they could get; you could almost see the pound signs dancing in their eyes. Even his ex-wife had been interested in his bank balance and his divorce settlement had cost him far more than he cared to think about.

Dione, on the other hand, didn't even seem to like him. Admittedly she had responded to his kiss, which he had thought a good sign. How wrong could a man be? It was nothing more than gratitude for helping her overcome her nightmare problem.

His lips thinned at the thought of Keristari wrenching her away from her mother at such a tender age. What a brute the man was; even worse than he'd always thought. He had ruined two lives with his selfishness. He was a totally uncaring swine of a man and Theo wished now that he'd never given him the money.

Except that he would never have got to know Dione if he hadn't! And he wouldn't be feeling her harsh rejection! Her outburst this morning had surprised him because he'd begun to think that he was getting somewhere. Now it looked as though he was back to square one.

He'd given her an ultimatum but he would never force himself on her. On the other hand, he knew that he couldn't live with her day in and day out and not even touch her. He would have to use all of his charm and wiles.

He smiled in satisfaction; he was going to enjoy it.

'I'm glad you find it amusing,' said Dione testily.

'Come on, Dione, don't be so uptight. We have a further twelve months to get through; you can't spend all of our time together hating me.'

'But I don't have to let you make love to me,' she retorted hastily. 'A deal's a deal as far as I'm concerned and you crossed the line last night.'

'You didn't stop me.' In fact, he felt sure she had enjoyed it as much as he had.

'I needed comfort.'

'But not the sort I offered?' he asked, his turn to speak sharply. 'You needn't answer that; you've made yourself very clear. Feel free to go to your mother's today if you want to.' And with that he walked out of the room.

Dione didn't stop to wonder why Theo had had a change of heart; it was sufficient that he had, and within the next twenty minutes she was hailing a taxi. But before he could even pull up Theo had driven into the space in front of her. 'Jump in.'

He was giving her no option and Dione slid into the seat beside him. 'Thank you,' she said quietly.

'You're welcome.'

It was a tight-lipped reply and Dione guessed he was angry with her for wanting to go off on her own. But she didn't care; she needed space, she needed time to sort out her muddled thoughts. Since the kiss she'd had mixed feelings about Theo, not least of which was the fact that she'd enjoyed it.

He dropped her off at her mother's, declaring that he'd pick her up again at twelve and take her to lunch. His words were brusque and Dione knew that she dared not argue.

Jeannie was surprised to see her again so soon and Dione hugged her warmly. 'I'm sorry you had to find out about Theo like that,' she apologised. 'It really did happen like I said. The instant we met we both knew we were meant for each other.'

'You could at least have phoned me,' said Jeannie, her hurt showing in her pained blue eyes.

'I could have,' admitted Dione, 'but I knew there wasn't time to fly you over—and I doubt you'd have come because of Yannis. It was Theo's idea that we tell you face to face. Do you like him?' she asked, trying to sound eager when in fact she was hurting inside at having to deceive her mother.

'He—seems very nice,' answered Jeannie, 'from what I've seen of him. He's very good-looking and has perfect manners. I hope he'll make you happy. I was happy with your father once, but he changed when we were married. I trust Theo won't do the same.'

Dione shook her head. 'He won't; he's a different person altogether from my father. He doesn't even like Yannis.'

'Not many people do,' Jeannie admitted. 'I'm surprised you've left him, considering he's still in hospital. What did he have to say about you marrying Theo?'

'He's happy for me.' Which wasn't a lie. Yannis was ecstatic, though she wasn't sure that he'd be entirely happy when he found out that they'd gone to England on their honeymoon. She had left Phrosini to tell him.

'Why am I not surprised?' asked Jeannie drily. 'He's always wanted you to marry one of his own. And now his wish has come true. Are you going to settle in Greece?'

'Theo's business is based there.'

'What does he do?'

'He owns a worldwide chain of hotels. I believe there's one in London.'

'So he's very rich?' Jeannie's tone was unusually disparaging.

Dione nodded. 'That's not why I married him, Mother, if that's what you're thinking.'

'Yannis' ambition was to be rich,' pointed out Jeannie. 'In my opinion it sours men. They have a very narrow view on the rest of the world. Don't let yourself get sucked into a trap.'

'Theo isn't like my father.'

'Are you sure?'

Dione nodded.

'Then I'm happy for you, my darling.'

Jeannie made some tea and they sat and talked some more until finally the subject of Chris was brought up.

'I never knew he could be like that,' said Dione.

'Me neither,' admitted her mother. 'It certainly opened my eyes. If he dares show his face here again I shall tell him exactly what I think of him.'

Dione smiled. Somehow she couldn't see her mother doing that, although there did seem to be a much stronger backbone in her today.

'Do you know what?' asked Jeannie. 'He actually asked if he could move in with me. Be my lodger. Apparently he's being thrown out of his flat.'

'You've not said yes?' asked Dione, appalled. It seemed to her that all Chris would be after was free food and lodgings.

Jeannie shook her head. 'In fact I always thought there was something odd about him, although for your sake I did try to like him. But I like Theo better,' she added with a smile. 'I'm glad to see that you're following your heart. I have my reservations, obviously, as it's all happened so quickly—but the same happened with your father and me. I fell in love with him at first sight.'

It was the first time her mother had told her this and Dione touched her hand. 'You think Theo will treat me badly?'

'I wouldn't be a caring parent if I didn't feel a little concerned, but on the surface he seems very nice.'

'He's much nicer than Chris,' said Dione forcefully. 'Do you know that just before I left for Greece I found out that Chris had been seeing his old girlfriend again?'

Jeannie shook her head. 'No, I didn't know that.'

'He denied it when I asked him. But my source was

very reliable. He had no right to say those things to me about marrying Theo when he'd already two-timed me behind my back.'

'How right you are,' said Jeannie. 'I wonder if he'll turn up for his lunch today?'

Dione's eyes shot wide. 'He wouldn't dare. Maybe I should wait and see, though. I don't want you tackling him on your own.'

'I can deal with Chris,' said her mother in a much more confident voice than usual. 'I've seen him now for what he is. You don't have to wait.'

Dione was shocked. Yannis had knocked her mother's self-confidence to such an extent that she rarely stood up for herself. This was an amazing turn-around. But still she hesitated about leaving her.

When Theo came to pick her up she opened the door to him. 'Would you mind coming back later?' she asked. 'I need to see Chris; he'll be here shortly.'

Theo's face darkened, and his eyes became bullets of steel. 'What for? What else is there to talk about?' he asked harshly.

About to tell him that it had nothing to do with their relationship, Dione changed her mind. 'There are things that need to be said,' she told him coolly.

'Perhaps I should stay and hear them?'

'And perhaps it's none of your business,' she snapped.

He met and held her eyes for several long seconds. It was a battle of wills and Dione had no intention of backing down. In the end he snarled, 'Very well.' And spun on his heel. Car tyres squealed as he sped away, and almost immediately Chris came around the other corner.

'Dione!' he exclaimed, alighting from his car. 'I

didn't expect to find you here. Was that your—er—
husband just leaving?'

She nodded briefly.

'What's happened? Fallen out already?' Chris' eyes
gleamed with delight.

'Nothing of the sort,' she told him shortly, leading the
way back into the house. 'My mother has something to
say to you and we thought it best done in private.'

Chris lifted his untidy brows.

Jeannie kept it short. 'I'm sorry to say this, Chris, but
you are no longer welcome in my house.'

He frowned and then glared at Dione. 'This is your
doing, isn't it? Now you're married to that man you
think you can dictate to your mother, tell her what to do.'

'It has nothing to do with my daughter's marriage,'
said Jeannie sharply. 'I've let you take me for a fool, but
not any longer. I want you to go, Chris, and I don't want
you to come back.'

Chris frowned, as astonished as Dione at the change
in her mother. And then he turned to Dione. 'What's
this, a conspiracy?'

'If you like to see it that way,' said Dione. 'My
mother and I both agree that it's no longer acceptable.'

'And guess who put the idea into your mother's
head,' he scorned. 'Well, thanks very much, Dione! First
you run off and marry the first rich man you meet, and
now you're banning me from this house. You're not the
girl I thought you were, Dione. Theo's welcome. He'll
soon find out what an unpleasant little witch you are.'

And with that he spun on his heel and left.

Dione and Jeannie looked at each other and smiled in
disbelief. When Theo turned up they were sitting sipping

tea. In contrast he looked far from happy. Dione promised her mother that she'd come to see her again before they left, and then followed her husband out to his car.

He drove silently and grimly but thankfully not at high speed. Dione felt his presence almost as much as when he had comforted her last night. Even though he was still angry it was overridden by his high sexuality. She could almost breathe in the passion inside him.

As they pulled up outside a private club the car was taken from him to be driven to some secret parking area, and Theo ushered her inside, where the atmosphere was hushed and opulent and everyone seemed to know everyone else.

Theo shrugged off their greetings and took Dione into a quiet corner of the dining room where their conversation would not be overheard. He came straight to the point.

'What was so important that you had to talk to that idiot of a boyfriend of yours without me being present?'

Dione glared. 'Chris is no longer my boyfriend.'

'Naturally,' snarled Theo. 'It was a mere figure of speech. But I hope you weren't telling him about our marriage, promising that once it's over you'll go back to him.'

If the fierce light in his eyes was supposed to frighten her, it didn't. Dione was used to men like him. 'No one has any idea about our arrangement, you can be sure of that. I wouldn't humiliate myself.'

'So you find being married to me humiliating?' he jeered, not looking pleased by the inference.

'What do you think?' she riposted, her dark eyes flashing her displeasure. 'Being forced into marriage wouldn't be anyone's idea of delight.'

'No one held a gun to your head,' he pointed out, at the same time indicating to a hovering wine waiter that they weren't yet ready to order.

'True,' Dione admitted, 'but it's what it feels like. I know I did it for my father, but I can't say that I'm getting any pleasure out of it.'

'You could if you tried.' His voice had gone a degree lower. 'You proved that last night. Tell me, did you respond to Chris' kisses the way you did to mine? Maybe you're not aware of it, but you revealed a hidden passion that it will be my pleasure to explore.'

'Never!' she cried, ignoring his question about Chris because the truth would have scared her. No one had lit her inner fire better than Theo. It both frightened and excited her at the same time. 'You're forgetting the terms of our contract.'

'Oh, I haven't forgotten, believe me.' His smile was wickedly assured. 'I'm simply assuming that one day passion will overtake us.'

Dione felt like striking out at him; at the same time she knew that what he said was true. She only had to let her guard slip once and he wouldn't hesitate to take advantage. When that happened she would be lost. 'You assume too much,' she told him testily.

'You're saying that you're not passionate? That you and Chris never made love until you felt that you were floating on a different planet?'

'What Chris and I did is none of your business,' she retorted angrily, at the same time feeling her cheeks flush. What would Theo think if he knew she was a virgin? Would he think her too pious for her own good? Would he call her an ice maiden as Chris had sometimes done? Chris hadn't been at all happy when she wouldn't go to bed with him, declaring that she was saving herself for when she got married.

And now she was married!

And she still didn't want to be made love to!

She was relieved when Theo beckoned the waiter and ordered their drinks. They studied the menu but she didn't know what she wanted, so Theo ordered for her. He had an alarming effect on her that at times made her feel strong and in control, and at others as weak as a kitten.

Damn the man for doing this to her!

'Have you any plans to see Chris again?'

The question took her by surprise. 'For your information, my mother's told him not to darken her doorstep again. I'm playing this game the way you want it.'

'So you see our marriage as a game?'

'Isn't it?' she thrust back. 'A game of power between you and my father! I hate the fact that I have been put in this position.'

Theo's brows rose and he leaned back in his chair and studied her, his dark eyes extremely intense, as though they were trying to look into her very soul. 'If you hate your father, why would you tie yourself to me for him?'

Dione immediately regretted her outburst. She did hate her father sometimes, but she loved him as well. And she would always be loyal to him. Perhaps he'd bullied her into thinking that way, but whatever she would never let him down. 'I didn't say I hated him altogether—only for what he's made me do. And I did it for his health's sake. I don't wish to discuss it any more.' She wished their meal would arrive so that she could concentrate on that instead.

'He's a very lucky man. And I'm lucky too to have such a delightful bride.' His black mood seemed to have left him and with a smile he reached across the table and took her hand.

Dione felt a whizz of something electric shoot through her arm, continuing into her body until it felt on fire. And all this because he had touched her! Hell, what was happening?

His thumb stroked and tormented and she wanted to snatch away; on the other hand she didn't want to give him the satisfaction of knowing that he disturbed her. Last night had been such a big mistake. She had appreciated him comforting her but she ought never to have let him kiss her. It had opened a door an inch and now his foot was in he wanted to take advantage.

During their meal they talked about everything except themselves, for which Dione was grateful. And by the time they had finished she was feeling more comfortable in his presence.

They walked afterwards, seeing the sights of London as though they were tourists. They took a boat trip down the Thames and a ride on the London Eye, exclaiming over the terrific views on such a clear day. And when they finally went back to his apartment Dione was tired but happy.

Theo had asked her no more awkward questions, made no untoward approaches apart from holding her hand, and if this was going to be his attitude for the rest of their so-called honeymoon then she could deal with it. She didn't dare think any further than that.

His housekeeper had dinner ready for them and after all their walking Dione had a good appetite. It was not until afterwards, when she and Theo were watching the darkening sky from the comfort of the balcony, Beethoven's Ninth playing in the background, that uneasiness began to assail her.

This was intimate; this was different from how it had been during the day. She could sense Theo looking at her instead of the view and wondered whether she ought to escape before it was too late. Or was she reading something that wasn't there?

'Doesn't London look beautiful at night?' she asked him.

'Not as lovely as you.'

She turned then and met the blackness of his eyes. 'You're not supposed to pay me compliments,' she said, alarmed to feel a sudden awareness. It was not easy ignoring this man's glances, especially when they expressed desire.

'Why? All women deserve compliments.'

'But our relationship is different,' she protested.

'Which makes it all the more exciting,' he growled. 'You're a very sexy woman, Dione.'

'And you're a smooth talker,' she flashed back, trying to ignore the fluttering of her heart. 'It won't get you anywhere.'

'Such a pity! I really would like to get somewhere with you.' The growl had deepened to a rumble within his chest and it was filled with innuendo.

Dione shot to her feet. 'This is a ridiculous conversation. I'm going to my room.'

'Not so quickly.' Theo's hand caught her arm as she jumped up. 'I've already promised that nothing will happen without your permission, so why the need to rush away?' And then he smiled, a devilish smile that revealed his wolfish white teeth and crinkled the corners of his eyes. 'Unless it's your own feelings that are running wild? Is that it, perhaps?'

'You're out of your mind,' snapped Dione. And she was out of hers because what he'd said was true. Pleasant hours spent in Theo's company had triggered emotions she would rather not feel.

'Mmm, I wonder,' he said in amusement. 'Sit down, Dione; you're going nowhere yet. I think you're forgetting that you're mine, and I happen to want your company for the rest of the evening. I have no wish to sit here alone.'

Although he was smiling there was a hard edge to his voice and, much against her better judgement, Dione dropped back into her chair. Damn the man. He was clearly used to getting his own way, and, fool that she was, she was allowing it. Why had she always thought that she could stand up to him?

She could have done if her weak body hadn't decided to respond. It was nothing to do with her head or her mind, it was her treacherous limbs, and all the nerves and pulses that were too sensitive for their own good.

Theo hitched his chair round so that he sat facing her, and, leaning forward, he took her hands into his. 'You have nothing to be afraid of, Dione. I'm not a big bad wolf.'

She tried to tug free but his grip was strong and in the end she gave in. A fatal mistake, because within seconds her heart raced out of control.

'We're in this together, you and I,' he growled. 'And twelve months is a long time if you're not enjoying yourself. If I were you, Dione, I'd stop fighting and start having fun.'

'It's different for you,' she flared, 'you're enjoying this situation; I'm not. Have you any idea what it was like telling my mother about us? I wonder what sort of a fool she took me for, marrying a man I hardly know.'

Theo shrugged. 'It looked to me as though she accepted the fact that it was love at first sight. You lied very convincingly, *agapi mou*. So convincingly, in fact, that I began to believe the story myself! Perhaps you are attracted to me, even though you deny it? Perhaps we should experiment again?'

'Don't you dare,' cried Dione in panic as his head drew closer to hers. But then she found that she could do nothing to stop him. With pounding heart, and a red-hot heat searing every limb, she allowed him to claim her lips in a kiss that set her soul on fire.

If he hadn't kissed her last night, if she hadn't felt the full portent of his kisses, she might have found the energy to reject him. But, fool that she was, she drank in every blissful second of it, and when he deepened the kiss, when he pulled her forward onto his lap, she did nothing to resist.

Beneath her she could feel the thundering heat of him and a throbbing readiness, and she wriggled uncontrollably, kissing him back, allowing her fingers to feel the harsh contours of his face and the shape of his head beneath the glossy dark hair.

'Ah, Dione, how I want you,' he breathed between kisses.

And Dione, to her shame, silently acknowledged that she wanted him too.

CHAPTER NINE

OUT HERE on this sultry summer evening Theo seemed more harshly Greek than ever, and he stirred her senses in a way no Englishman ever could. Despite all her reservations about marrying a native of her father's country, Dione could feel herself being drawn towards this vital, arrogantly handsome man in a way she had never expected.

Her nipples hardened and tingled as they brushed against the explosive hardness of his chest, and, ignoring warnings echoing repeatedly in the back of her mind, Dione sucked in his kisses, her tongue meeting his eagerly and sensually. She was giving all the wrong signals, she was very aware of that, but the will-power to move was non-existent.

The kiss grew deeply intimate and their individual body heat moulded into one smouldering fire. His fingertips touched and stroked the bare flesh on her arms and throat, igniting flames, and Dione wriggled uncontrollably, conscious of the heat between her thighs and her desperate need for fulfilment.

Never before had she felt such an urge, never felt the need to break her self-imposed vows. It became crystal clear in her mind that Theo was an expert in the art of seduction, far more passionate than any Englishman she'd been out with—and yet she'd been certain that she would marry one. Greeks had been entirely off her agenda.

On the other hand, it didn't mean that she was falling in love with Theo. This was nothing more than chemical attraction. But what an attraction! Desire meeting desire—though where hers had come from Dione had no idea. Fire meeting fire! Animal hunger meeting animal hunger! Whichever way she worded it, it all amounted to the same thing.

She wanted Theo!

It was a new and alien feeling, a stimulation of her senses, anticipation of the unknown, of the sheer enormity of aroused feelings. She'd been called an ice maiden many times and now she knew why. No one had ever managed to intoxicate her into feeling heady with an aching bodily need.

When she gave a shiver of pleasure Theo stopped kissing and looked at her with concern. 'Are you cold, *agapi mou*?'

She replied with the merest shake of her head, her throat so tight that she could not speak.

Nevertheless Theo swung her up into his arms. 'Somewhere more comfortable, I think.'

Dione knew that she ought to protest; there was still a sane part of her mind that told her she would despise herself tomorrow morning if she let Theo have his way. But insanity ruled. She allowed him to carry her to his bedroom and lay her down on the bed.

'This is OK for you?' he asked gruffly. 'I don't want you to do anything that you'll regret.'

In response Dione linked her hands behind his neck and pulled his face down to hers. Nothing else mattered at this moment of madness except feeling Theo inside her! The ache in her groin, the desperate need, would not go away until it had been assuaged by this spectacularly sexy man—who also happened to be her husband!

Whether it was this thought that made it all right in her mind Dione could not be sure; all she knew was that she wanted him to make love to her. *Now!* Never in her life had she felt such an intense ache in the pit of her stomach, or the honeyed sweetness that moistened the sexual heart of her.

She felt Theo's groan vibrate through the length of his body, and with excruciating slowness he popped the buttons on her blouse. Dione's breasts burgeoned and ached as inch by inch her flesh was revealed, and they seemed to lift themselves of their own volition for his touch.

A further tiny groan escaped him as he stroked and explored, easing his fingers inside her bra to squeeze her nipples in an exquisite taste of what was to come, before rolling her on her side so that he could flick it undone and whisk it away. A smile settled on his lips, one of pure pleasure and anticipation, his eyes feasting themselves on her curves.

When finally her breasts were exposed his eyes grew even darker as he sucked each of them in turn urgently into his mouth. Dione's body arched involuntarily, her hands gripping his head, fingers tugging at his hair, her hips gyrating as wave after wave of desperate need flowed through her.

But Theo was in no hurry. It was a deliberate, slow

seduction of her senses, bringing her further and further into the realms of no return. She heard her voice saying his name over and over like a mantra.

'This is good?' he asked, raising his eyes to hers, his lips moist and soft as he hovered millimetres above her tingling breasts.

She nodded. 'I don't know what you're doing to me but I want more.'

'You and me both,' he rasped, and his actions became more urgent, his hands moving to her skirt now to slide it down over her hips, revealing white lacy panties that matched her bra.

They felt damp and she was embarrassed as he slithered them off. 'Now you're all mine.'

There was a hot intensity in his wicked dark eyes, and with the frenetic energy of a man possessed he whipped off his own clothes and leapt on the bed beside her. All of a sudden it wasn't a matter of persuasion and seduction, it was a feverish hunger that needed assuaging—right now!

Dione had no time to feel afraid; her fingers tightened over Theo's shoulders as he drove himself into her. He hesitated only briefly when he felt resistance, but there was no going back. He could not stop, nor did she want him to. They were both being carried away by their own heated desire.

Her climax, when it came, sent her spinning into outer space. She was unprepared for the waves of sensation that pounded through her body, that made her gasp time and time again, her heart beating so loudly she felt sure that it could be heard all over the building.

She wanted to cling on to Theo, who was experiencing the same mind-bending convulsions, but he turned abruptly away when she touched him and rolled off the bed. His body was slicked with sweat but he regained his composure before she did and his voice was full of anger when he finally spoke.

'Why the hell didn't you tell me that you were a virgin?'

Dione swallowed hard, taken aback by his harsh words. He was spoiling a beautiful moment, didn't he know that? She had always wanted her first time to be special, and up until this point it had been. Now he was defiling it. 'If it doesn't matter to me, why does it matter to you?' she demanded, pulling a sheet over her still aching body.

'Dammit, Dione, it does matter. I would never have taken you so roughly had I known.'

'I'm not complaining,' she returned, getting up also and hugging the sheet around her.

Theo didn't seem to notice that he was still nude, that he wore nothing except a scowl. 'But I don't like it. I've never done that to a woman in my life.'

'Didn't you enjoy it?' she challenged, suddenly beginning to feel degraded.

'Of course I damn well enjoyed it—that isn't the point.' His tone suddenly changed to one of concern. 'Are you all right?'

Dione nodded. 'I just need a shower.' And, feeling utterly humiliated now, she hurried over to the adjoining door and slammed it shut behind her.

Theo let out a harsh breath. Damn! The worst thing was that he hadn't been able to control himself. He had known what he was doing, he had recognised that Dione was a virgin, and yet he hadn't stopped. What sort of a swine must she take him for?

His body still raged with rampant hormones and yet he had never been so angry with himself. Dione had said it didn't matter, but he had taken her without thought for her feelings.

He could never make love to her again because this moment would come back to haunt him. She'd felt so fantastic in his arms—she had the body of an angel and he'd felt hidden fires within her; he'd even begun to look forward to long, sensual nights spent together in bed.

If only she'd told him she was a virgin things could have been so different. He would have treated her with the tenderness she deserved; he would have enjoyed initiating her into acts of love. Instead…

Theo's shoulders drooped as he headed for his own shower. A long, cold shower, but it did nothing to lessen his anger. And he wasn't looking forward to speaking to Dione again. Somehow he would have to bluff his way out of it, not let her see how much his mistake had affected him.

She had put on a brave face, pretended it didn't matter, but he knew how much a woman's virginity meant to her, especially a woman of Dione's age. Clearly she had been saving herself for Mr Right, maybe even Chris Donovan, had they married, and now he had taken it.

Never in his life had he hated himself as much as he did at that moment, and when he heard the key turn in the door between their two rooms his heart sank even further.

Dione couldn't sleep. She had gone to bed telling herself that she didn't care, but deep within her heart she struggled to come to terms with what had happened. It wasn't as though it was solely Theo's fault. She was as much to blame. They had fallen on each other like two sex-starved animals, something she had never imagined herself doing!

On the other hand, perhaps it was a good thing that Theo was disappointed in himself. It might keep him away from her in future; because if they continued to make love during the whole of their twelve-month contract then one of them, maybe both, might find it hard to part at the end of the term.

Finally Dione fell into a dreamless sleep and woke feeling more at ease with herself—until a horrific thought struck her. What if she was pregnant? Theo had been too impatient to use protection and she hadn't even thought about it. Could it happen the first time? She was ashamed to admit that she didn't know. She could only hope not and she had no intention of passing any of her fears on to Theo.

They met over breakfast and both of them studiously avoided mentioning what had happened last night. Theo wore a white polo shirt and black chinos and Dione had chosen a simple beige dress with an orange and brown pattern. Had she subconsciously dressed to suit their mood? she couldn't help wondering.

Her mood was definitely brown and she wondered what plans Theo had for the day. If they'd been an ordinary newly wed couple they would probably have spent all their time in bed, never leaving the apartment, but due to their extreme circumstances this was hardly likely to be the case.

Theo looked as though he'd had a sleepless night as

well, with shadows beneath his eyes and his hair all over the place. 'What are we doing today?' she asked, partly to break the silence, partly because it would be good to know what he had planned.

'I think a good, long walk in Hyde Park might be the answer,' he declared. 'Blow the cobwebs away. Do you horse-ride? We could do that if you like.'

Dione shook her head. 'No, I don't.' And if she did it would have been uncomfortable sitting astride a saddle. Not that he'd think of that. What man would?

But he amazed her by pulling a rueful face. 'Sorry, wrong question to ask. Are you terribly sore?'

'I'm OK,' she lied.

He shook his head in anger at himself. 'I was stupid. I got carried away. Do forgive me.'

'Let's forget the whole issue,' said Dione hastily, although she appreciated his apology. 'What's done is done. I've finished. Let's go.'

Amazingly they enjoyed themselves, both making a determined effort to put the events of last night behind them. 'I guess this isn't how you usually spend your day?' queried Dione as they rested on a park bench after walking for a good hour and a half. They had spent their time chatting, pointing out different things of interest…a grey squirrel, a robin, blackbirds, ducks; anything that caught their attention.

Anything other than themselves!

'Indeed not,' he agreed, smiling into her face for the first time that morning. 'I'm usually dashing here, there and everywhere; my feet hardly touch the ground. I can't remember the last time I took a break like this.'

When Theo smiled, when his face softened and his

eyes crinkled, Dione forgot the atmosphere between them and felt a fresh surge of awareness. It was foolishness, she knew, and she kept it well-hidden. 'You should be ashamed,' she admonished instead. 'Everyone needs to relax some time.'

Theo shrugged his magnificent shoulders. 'I'll be the first to admit it. But running a business like mine doesn't leave much time for relaxation.'

'Am I right in believing you have a hotel here in London?'

'I do. One of my finest,' he answered proudly.

'Can I see it?'

Theo looked at her with raised brows. 'If you're really interested.'

'Of course.'

He looked pleased. 'Then I'll take you there tomorrow.'

After that the atmosphere between them seemed to lighten, and by the end of the day they were chatting like the best of friends. Dione knew that she ought to be pleased, that this was what she had wanted from the very beginning, but after last night, after he had sent her soaring with the stars, how could she be happy with a platonic relationship? Her whole body felt different. More alive, more feminine, more everything, in fact. She even wanted to be made love to again.

But it was not to be. After another of his housekeeper's scrumptious meals—poached salmon with garden peas and tiny new potatoes—Theo took a phone call in his study and when he came back his face was grim.

'I have to return home. Some damn idiot's hacked

into our computer system and has downloaded personal information.'

Dione frowned. 'And you're expected to sort it?'

'Not me personally—the police have been called in—but I naturally want to be there. It affects the whole company; we could be in big trouble. We're leaving in an hour. I've asked Mary to pack our cases.'

'I could have done that,' she protested but he was hardly listening. She could see his brain working overtime; she was non-existent at this moment. 'Would it help if I stayed here?' she asked hesitantly. 'Then you can go straight to your office.'

Dark eyes pierced her. 'And leave you to the likes of Chris Donovan? Not on your life. You're coming whether you want to or not.'

It was a silent journey in Theo's private jet. His thoughts were on what was happening and he seemed hardly to notice her existence. It should have suited her just fine except that she would have liked to be involved. She would have liked him to talk to her about it, share his thoughts and fears.

Two cars were waiting at the airport, one to whisk Theo to his office and another to take her home and, although she'd missed a night's sleep and went straight to bed, all Dione could think about was Theo's problem. She might have been forced into this marriage but even in these few days he had become a big part of her life and she was truly concerned for him.

Later in the morning she went to see her father and found him sitting up in his hospital bed, much improved.

'I have you to thank for this, my loyal daughter,' he said. 'How is married life? Is Theo looking after you?'

'Of course; he's very much a gentleman,' she answered, marvelling that her father could speak about it as though it were a proper marriage.

'Not too much of a gentleman, I hope?' he asked with a knowing twinkle in his eye. 'You are—sharing a bed?'

'I think what we do is none of your business,' retorted Dione, speaking more sharply than she usually did to her father. 'You got your money—isn't that enough? Where's Phrosini?'

'You've just missed her. But she'll be back; you'll see her later.'

'I'm not staying that long, Father.' She thought of telling him about Theo's problem but then decided against it. Knowing Yannis, he would gloat. So long as his business was picking up he really cared little about anyone else.

'I expected you to be away longer than this,' he said.

'You know Theo,' she said; 'he's like you—he can't keep away from his work.'

'But you're not entirely unhappy?'

As if he cared! Nevertheless Dione shook her head. 'We get on well under the circumstances.'

'Will he mind you still working for me?'

'What?' Dione's eyes shot wide. 'You can't expect me to carry on after you've sold me to him?'

'*Dione!*' Yannis sounded scandalised by her suggestion, his face more animated than she had seen it in a long time.

'Isn't that what you did?' she tossed angrily. 'Sold me! I don't belong to you any more. I'm glad you're getting better but believe me, I shan't be visiting you on a daily basis. In fact, you deserve no visits at all.' It was the first time she had ever spoken to her father like this but something inside her had snapped and she actually felt relief. Maybe he had done her a favour after all?

CHAPTER TEN

THEO didn't even phone. Dione waited all day to hear how things were going and was hurt when he didn't contact her. Maybe he thought it was none of her business.

When he did finally come home it was almost midnight and she was in bed. Though not asleep! She had lain there listening for him, feeling more lonely than at any other time in her life. In the four days since their marriage she had grown used to his presence, had even begun to feel comfortable with him, and she missed him as she had never expected.

Pulling on a white towelling robe over her skimpy nightie, Dione made her way downstairs. Theo sat stretched out in a chair in the massive living area, a glass of whisky in his hand, looking so strained and tired that her heart went out to him. She flew across the room. 'Theo, how are things?'

He looked at her with red-rimmed eyes. 'We're getting there. What are you doing up at this time of night?'

'I've been worried about you,' she declared honestly.

'Why?'

'Why?' she echoed. 'Because…' She had been about to say 'because you're my husband'. But that would infer that theirs was a proper marriage and she loved and cared about him, and that wasn't the way of things at all. 'Because it's a horrible thing to happen to anyone. Is it very bad?'

'It could be worse if it hadn't been spotted. But it's going to involve many hours of work and could set the company back months. The police are working on it, thank goodness.'

'Do you think I could be of any help?' asked Dione. 'I'm completely computer savvy.'

'You are?'

She nodded.

'Didn't you tell me that you were an interior designer and that you worked for your father?'

'I did, but not any more.'

Well-marked brows rose.

'I went to see him today and told him so.'

'Good for you!' he exclaimed. 'I bet he wasn't happy.'

Dione shrugged. 'I said that since he'd sold me to you I owed him nothing.'

A harsh frown slashed Theo's brow but he didn't deny that he owned her and, although it shouldn't have done, Dione found it deeply hurtful. Somehow, since the night he'd made love to her, she'd felt differently towards him, and she had thought that maybe he had too. Not love, nothing like that, but more a friendship than an arrangement written on a piece of paper.

His non-answer confirmed that he didn't see it that way. He had bought her to do with as he wished. And if he chose to ignore her for twenty-four hours at a time it was something she had to put up with.

'You look tired,' she said, changing the conversation. 'Why don't you go to bed?'

'And you think I'd sleep?' he scoffed. 'Go back yourself, Dione; there's nothing you can do.'

Hiding her hurt, Dione turned and made her way upstairs. If that was the way Theo chose to play it there was nothing she could do. She lay listening for him to turn in too, but in the end she was asleep before he did. And the next morning he was gone when she woke up.

Instead she had a visitor. 'Mrs Tsardikos, it's Mrs Tsardikos,' said Theo's housekeeper with what sounded like an apology. 'I've put her in the living room.'

Dione frowned, wondering why Theo's mother had chosen to pay her a visit.

But the glamorous woman who turned to face her as she entered the room was not her mother-in-law but a complete stranger, and for the first few seconds she stared at Dione without speaking.

'I'm Theo's first wife, Katina,' she announced finally. But she didn't extend a hand of greeting. 'And you're the next fool.'

Dione frowned. 'I beg your pardon?' The woman was handsome in a hard sort of way, with her hair beautifully coiffed and her make-up perfect. The harsh red colour of her lips was echoed in her fingernails, but the black suit she wore made her look very severe.

'I felt it my place to come and warn you in case you don't realise exactly what you've let yourself in for.'

'I think,' said Dione, hating her on sight, 'that that's my business and nothing at all to do with you.' The woman was overbearing. It was no wonder their marriage hadn't lasted.

'Theo can be the perfect gentleman on the outside,' continued his ex-wife, as though Dione hadn't spoken, 'but he's a complete swine otherwise. I wouldn't wish him on my worst enemy.'

'I've seen none of it so far,' countered Dione.

'That's why I'm here so early in your marriage,' came the glib response. 'If you take my advice you'll get out of it as quickly as you can.'

Dione stared hostilely at her visitor, scarcely able to believe what she was hearing. 'I don't need any advice, especially from you.'

'What's he been saying about me?' came the quick and almost fearful response.

'Nothing!' spat Dione. 'But exes are always hostile. It's natural. Thank you for coming but I'll wait and find out for myself what Theo's like.'

'You're making a big mistake,' purred Katina, perching on the edge of one of the chairs, clearly not yet prepared to leave. 'In twelve months' time you'll be wishing you'd listened and done something about it. Please ask Anna to make me a coffee.'

'I'm sorry!' exclaimed Dione with exaggerated politeness. 'I'm forgetting my manners. Please excuse me.' Outside the room she felt like spitting fire. She wasn't in the least sorry that she hadn't offered this insufferable woman a drink. What had Theo ever seen in her?

It took her several moments to regain her composure and return to the room, and as they sat drinking coffee she willed the other woman to leave.

'You had an amazingly short honeymoon,' said Katina complacently. 'What happened?

'Are you trying to tell me that you've been keeping

tabs on us?' asked Dione indignantly. She was shocked to hear that the woman knew so much.

'Tabs? What are tabs?' Her English was good but clearly there were words she was not familiar with.

'Checking up on us. To hear you talk you're thankful to be rid of Theo. Why the interest now?'

'It's you I'm thinking of.'

Dione tossed her head, her eyes flashing anger. 'I don't think so. Something tells me that you'd like Theo back. You're trying to get rid of me, that's what you're doing.'

'I wouldn't marry Theo again if he got down on his knees and begged,' scorned Katina.

But Dione didn't believe her. If she wasn't interested in him, why would she be here? The story about warning her what Theo was like didn't ring true. She was out to cause trouble.

'He's a womaniser. He might have married you but you're not the only one in his life. Have you ever wondered why he spends so much time at work? It's nothing more than a cover-up.'

'Really?' asked Dione. 'And you have proof of this, do you? Perhaps he did it when he was married to you but our marriage is different.' In a way that Katina would never know about. 'He won't cheat on me.'

'You sound so sure that I pity you,' scorned Theo's ex. 'But of course you've only been married a short time. I was confident of him once. And look what happened when we lost our child—you did know about that?'

Dione nodded.

'He saw it as an excuse and left. He blamed it on me, of course. Said I'd changed, but the truth is Theo doesn't want to be tied down. You're nothing more to him than a novelty. If I were you I'd get out of this marriage before he throws you out.'

'I'm sorry,' said Dione stiffly, unable to remain civil any longer, 'I don't remember asking for your advice.'

'It's freely given,' said Katina, putting down her empty cup and standing up. 'Do tell Theo I called. I'll see myself out.' And she sailed from the room.

Dione was so angry that she couldn't rest and when Theo came home later that evening the first thing she did was tell him about his ex-wife's visit.

'She had no right coming here,' he roared, his eyes flashing golden anger. 'You should have phoned me. I would have come right over and told her to leave. Did she upset you?'

As if he cared! Dione didn't even deign to answer.

'What did she want?'

Dione lifted her shoulders in a helpless little shrug. 'To warn me against you!'

Theo's face became suffused with colour and he let out a hiss of rage. 'I wonder who the hell told her we'd got married.'

'I guess it's common knowledge,' acknowledged Dione wryly. The wedding had been no secret. In fact, it had been a far bigger ceremony than she would have liked under the circumstances, though she had never told Theo that. 'But I am interested as to why she would tell me you weren't a fit husband. Is there anything I don't know? Do you fly into fits of rage? Is my life in danger?'

'You know damn well it's not,' he thundered. 'Did you tell her about us?'

'Am I a fool?' she riposted. 'I may as well let you

know now I didn't like Katina. I can't think what you ever saw in her.'

'I sometimes wonder that myself,' he acknowledged quietly.

'She was clearly here to make trouble.'

'But you didn't let her get to you?'

Dione shook her head.

'If she ever comes again I want you to tell me straight away. In fact, I might go and see her. She had no right talking to you like that.'

'It's not worth it,' insisted Dione. 'She didn't get the better of me.'

'I'm glad you stood up to her,' said Theo.

'I'm not like my mother,' acknowledged Dione.

'I guess you've had years of practice with your father?' There was a wry twist to his lips as he spoke. 'Yannis is the biggest bully I know.'

'I agree,' she answered, 'and if he wasn't my father I wouldn't give him the time of day. But blood's thicker than water, isn't that what they say? He's given me a good upbringing... I've never been short of anything; I couldn't turn my back on him.'

'You're an amazing woman, Dione. Come here.' And he beckoned her to him.

Warily she approached and when he pulled her down onto his lap she made no attempt to resist. She could feel the good, strong beat of his heart against her side, and even after a long, hard day at work he still smelled good. The male scent of him was like an aphrodisiac and awareness sizzled through her with the speed of lightning.

'I went to see him today,' she said, trying to pretend

that it was quite normal to be sitting on his lap. 'He looks much better.'

'As well he should be,' snarled Theo, his mood changing. 'He got what he wanted.'

And you didn't, she was tempted to ask, when you were the one who gave the ultimatum? I was piggy in the middle. But she kept her thoughts to herself. 'Do you have any regrets?' she asked instead.

'Ask me that in six months' time,' he growled. 'Our marriage so far has been anything but smooth.'

'Did you expect it to be?' she enquired, wondering how they could be having such a conversation when hot desire filled her body.

'I didn't expect to have to fight off a jealous boy-friend,' he told her accusingly.

'And I didn't expect to have to deal with an ex-wife.' she retaliated.

'*Touché!* But it can't have been jealousy on her side because she was the one who walked out.'

'You never told me about her, though,' insisted Dione, finding it easier to ignore the tight tension inside her while talking about his ex.

'Why should I have done?' he asked harshly. 'This is hardly a marriage made in heaven, where both sides confess their past so that no skeletons turn up. There was nothing in our contract that said we needed to bare all.'

And then his voice lowered almost to a growl. 'I didn't ask you over here to talk about our past loves. It's the present I'm interested in. I need you, Dione, and I need you now.'

His arms tightened around her and his frank confession sent a further thrill spiralling through Dione's overheated veins. She tightened muscles in a vain endeavour to stem the hot hunger that stung the very heart of her and was almost afraid to look into his eyes in case he saw her very real need.

What she saw, though, was a question, one she hadn't expected, not after the last time. She had thought he would now take it as his right to make love to her whenever he felt like it. Unless, of course, he was asking whether it was still too soon?

Well, damn the soreness; she wanted him—badly. And he must have seen the answer in her eyes because with a groan he nuzzled the side of her neck, biting gently, sucking, kissing, moving his lips inexorably closer to her mouth.

Dione clutched his head, moaning her acceptance, her pleasure, her hunger. And her lips were parted and ready when he began his invasion. 'This is what a man needs after a hard day,' he muttered into her mouth. 'The sweet taste of woman! Someone to make him forget his worries.' His breathing grew harder, his voice more hoarse and his demands of her deeper.

The pulse in Dione's throat beat so hard it threatened to choke her, and her heart struggled to keep up with the demands made on it. By now she was putty in Theo's arms and when he snapped the straps on her nightie in his urgency to suck her stinging nipples into his mouth she felt nothing but extreme exhilaration.

His long fingers cupped her breasts, moulding and firming, and his teeth nipped and grazed, and when he looked up to judge her reaction his eyes were glazed. All worries over work had vanished and he was lost in a world where only senses mattered.

Dione wasn't aware of the moment that her night-dress had fallen even lower, conscious only that his fingers had blazed a trail over the flatness of her stomach and were now playing with the moistness between her thighs. He was incredibly gentle, but in so doing he was arousing her more than if he had taken her with urgency as he had before.

When she could stand it no longer, when her whole body writhed and wriggled and demanded fulfilment, when she cried out in both pleasure and despair, he swung her to her feet.

'Don't move,' he warned as he ripped his shirt over his head and removed his trousers. When he was glori-ously, excitingly naked he pulled her to him again and she felt him against her, and this time it was she who hooked her arms around his neck and pulled his head down to hers, all the time moving her body sensually against him.

'God, woman, what are you doing to me?' he groaned hoarsely. 'I can't stand any more of this.'

With the slickness of experience he turned her back on him, at the same time sliding a condom into place. Dione was thankful, even though she wouldn't have found the strength to stop him making love to her even if he hadn't. Never before had she felt such a powerful need. Her whole body throbbed and ached so much that it almost hurt.

His hands captured her sensitive breasts, fingers teasing aching nipples as he edged her towards a leather sofa. There he bent her forwards over the back of it and the coolness of the leather felt like heaven to her hot skin. Slowly he entered her from behind, constantly asking whether he was hurting, but each time she shook her head, completely incapable of speaking.

Even when she had taken the full length of him he still didn't rush. He took it slowly and sensually, riding her like a fine thoroughbred mare, until in the end it was Dione who begged for more.

'Faster, Theo, faster,' she cried. 'I can't stand any more of this.'

He was quick to obey and Dione shot to a climax a couple of seconds before Theo. Her knees gave way and they both ended up on the floor, heaving and writhing, gasping and groaning, feeling as though they'd died and gone to heaven. Finally, their limbs still heavy, they lay still.

'That was good for you, *agapi mou*?'

It was more than good—it had been out of this world, but did she want to admit that? What would she be letting herself in for? 'I never knew that making love could be so enervating,' she confessed with a wry smile.

Theo's skin glistened in the light from one of the floor lamps, and even in repose he still looked imposing. Naked or dressed, aroused or relaxed, he was one hell of an exciting male. She had never thought that when she agreed to marry him, had never expected that within a few short days she would be begging him to make love to her.

She had thought that the next twelve months were going to be hell; instead it looked as though she was going to enjoy them!

CHAPTER ELEVEN

IN THE weeks that followed Dione and Theo grew closer than she had ever expected. Not that she didn't always keep uppermost in her mind the fact that this was a temporary arrangement. Theo was still worried over his company affairs, though the police had traced and apprehended the hacker, who, it turned out, was a disgruntled ex-employee, but other than that they spent all of their spare time together.

She slept in his bed; they made love so many times that to even think about it embarrassed Dione. He teased her by saying that she had become obsessed by sex, but he also declared that he was one hell of a satisfied man. 'Persuading you to marry me was one of the best moves I've made,' he said one evening after a particularly long and satisfying love session.

Dione wasn't so sure. 'I hope you're not thinking of extending the twelve months. A contract is a contract, don't ever forget that.' She didn't want him getting any wrong ideas.

When Theo made love he was being driven by lust rather than any real feelings; and if she was honest with herself it was the same for her. It was amazing sex, but that was all it was; she could never see herself tied to Theo for the rest of her life.

Theo frowned. 'I'm a man of my word, Dione. 'You'll be free to fly when the time comes.'

When one morning she woke up feeling ill Dione thought it must have been the fish they'd had for supper the previous evening. But when it happened again, and she added up the dates, she knew that her worst nightmare had just become reality. She was pregnant!

And she was trapped! Trapped to a Greek man just as her mother had been! The very thought made her feel ill all over again.

Theo always left for the office before Dione got up and as yet he had no idea of the fear consuming her. Nor did she want to tell him because she wasn't feeling strong enough to deal with it herself just yet.

'Are you all right, Dione? You look pale.' They were sitting outside by the pool one evening, letting their meal go down, and Dione had closed her eyes. She felt guilty about not telling Theo; on the other hand she feared his anger more and intended putting off the evil moment for as long as she could.

'I'm fine,' she said, looking into surprisingly concerned brown eyes and hoping she was actress enough to get away with it.

'Perhaps you're not getting out enough? What do you do with yourself while I'm at work?'

Dione couldn't believe he was really interested. All that seemed to matter to him was that she was ready and waiting when he got home. There wasn't a single night when he didn't want to make love. His virility continually amazed her. Though she was forced to accept that her own needs were pretty much on a par with his. And this she found even more astounding.

'Not very much,' she acknowledged. 'I almost wish I hadn't given up my job with my father. I'm not cut out to be a stay-at-home wife.'

She swam sometimes but she didn't like sitting out in the sun. She had her father's dark hair but her mother's fair skin and burnt easily. She spent much of her time reading, or surfing the internet on a computer Theo had made available for her. She visited Phrosini and her father, but all her friends were at work during the day. It was very much a life of leisure but it wasn't for her.

'Maybe I should introduce you to some of my friends' wives. They seem to spend all their time shopping or at each other's houses.'

'No, thank you,' said Dione quickly. 'There are only ten months left; I'll get by.'

A harsh frown attacked Theo's brow. 'You're counting?'

'Wouldn't you in my position?' she snapped.

'Maybe I'm wrong, but I thought you were settled and happy. You always seem pleased to see me when I get home.'

Dione lifted narrow shoulders but said nothing. Her pleasure was purely sexual; even Theo should know that.

He snorted angrily and, jumping to his feet, he marched indoors. Dione spent that night in her own bed. She oughtn't to have spoken to him so rudely, she realised, because now life would be unbearable.

The following morning Theo had gone off to work and she was retching over the toilet as usual, when she heard a sound. Glancing over her shoulder, she saw her husband watching her. She slammed a tissue to her mouth and spun to face him, her eyes wide orbs of guilt.

'Does this mean what I think it means?' he asked harshly.

Dione nodded. No need for words; he was as angry as she had expected him to be.

'Why didn't you tell me?'

'Why are you spying on me?' she riposted furiously.

'I forgot something. And it looks as though it's lucky I did. You're pregnant?'

He made it sound like an accusation.

'And if I am, whose fault is it?' she demanded.

'Needless to say, I take precautions,' he shot back. 'And needless to say also, you've given no indication that you don't enjoy it. In fact, your appetite is as great as mine.'

'Maybe it is,' she agreed, 'so it must have happened on that first occasion. You didn't care then that you might get me pregnant. All you wanted to do was satisfy your own carnal urges.'

Theo closed his eyes and she could almost hear him counting to ten. And actually she had no right being angry because she was just as much to blame. 'Have you seen a doctor?'

Dione shook her head, and then wished she hadn't because the room spun round. Instantly Theo was at her side, a strong arm supporting her. With his other hand he filled a glass with water and bade her take a sip.

Her mouth felt putrid and she gladly took it off him.

'That's better,' he said eventually. 'You're looking more like your normal self now. Go back to bed. I'll send for my physician.'

'I'm not ill,' she protested vehemently.

'Then I'll take you to see him. I don't suppose you've had your pregnancy confirmed?'

Dione hated him fussing. 'I'll go in my own good time,' she retorted, 'to my own doctor.'

Theo nodded grimly. 'Will you be all right if I leave you now? I have something important to take care of.'

Tell me something different, thought Dione. But it was a relief to have him go. A relief also that he had found out about the baby.

Dione wasn't looking forward to Theo coming home that evening. Usually she bathed and made herself ready for him, but now she suspected there would be a change in their relationship.

'What's the matter with you, Theo? You haven't been yourself today. Not trouble with your wife already?'

Theo looked at his colleague and managed a wry smile. 'Not at all; she's everything a man could wish for.' Except that now, because of his own stupidity, she was having his baby. The very thought was sheer hell.

'There's obviously something on your mind,' insisted Dimitri. 'Can I help?'

'You can keep your nose out of it,' rasped Theo, and immediately regretted his outburst when he saw the man's dismay.

Theo always had a good relationship with his employees; he treated them fairly and kindly and they respected him for it. It was rare that he ever needed to tell anyone off. And Dimitri was his right-hand man; he knew as much about the business as Theo did. It was wrong to take his anger out on him.

He clapped a hand on Dimitri's shoulder. 'I shouldn't

have said that. It's true, I do have a problem, but it's personal and I don't wish to talk about it.'

His colleague shrugged. 'That's your prerogative, Theo. But if you do need an ear you know nothing will go any further.'

Theo nodded.

He couldn't even begin to describe his shock when he had seen Dione vomiting and he'd immediately known the reason for it. Hadn't Katina been exactly the same? And hadn't she tried to hide it from him as well?

Her excuse was that their marriage had been going through a bad patch and she had thought he'd be angry. As if! What man could be angry when he'd procreated a child, especially in wedlock? A child was born to be loved and cared for. To be guided through life, to be taught values.

A child did not die at a very young age!

Thoughts came tumbling back and Theo had to blink back tears and push them away. They did not bear thinking about.

But what was Dione's excuse for not telling him? Had she too been afraid that he'd be angry? Was he really that unapproachable? Their relationship had gone up several notches recently and he had begun to think that something more serious was developing.

And now she wanted to shut him out!

Which proved only one thing. That Dione's view of their relationship was entirely different from his. In her eyes their marriage was no more real now than it had been on the day they wed.

And by impregnating her with his seed he had ruined her life!

He couldn't bear the thought that he had hurt her a second time and knew that he had to go home and try to put matters right. Difficult, under the circumstances, but somehow he had to try. He needed to reassure her that he would never desert her, that he would see her through this, make sure she never suffered. Even if she didn't want to remain married to him he would give her every support possible.

When he got home he found her lying in the shade by the pool wearing nothing more than a skimpy black bikini. There was no evidence yet of her pregnancy; she was stunningly slender and beautiful, and his male hormones swung into appreciative action.

She lifted wide, surprised eyes to his face and she was clearly not happy to see him. 'What are you doing here at this time of day?'

'Have you seen the doctor?' he countered, ignoring her question.

'Not yet.'

'Have you phoned for an appointment?'

'No.'

'Why the hell not?' His voice rose in accordance with his frustration. He had so wanted to comfort Dione, to reassure her that he would take care of everything, but the vibes coming from her were not conducive to kind words.

'Because I didn't realise it was so important,' she defended. 'Is that why you're here, to make sure I carry out your wishes?' She stood up now and faced him, hands on her hips, her chin thrust out.

'I'm here because it's my fault you're in this condition.'

'At least you've got something right,' she countered furiously.

'And I want to take care of you.'

'Because it's the honourable thing to do?' she replied. 'Thanks, but no thanks; I don't need your help. It has never been my intention to stay with you a day longer than necessary and nothing has changed.'

And she meant it!

And she looked beautiful in her anger. So gorgeous, in fact, that he wanted to wrap his arms around her and kiss her senseless. 'For heaven's sake, go and make yourself decent,' he rasped. Damn the woman, she'd got beneath his skin in a way he'd never expected. What had started as a game was turning into something much more serious.

Dione needed no second bidding; she scuttled into the house as though an army of ants was chasing her. Theo slung his jacket over the back of a chair, took off his tie and undid his collar. He'd been cool in the car, but now the full heat of the midday sun bore down on him and he'd have liked nothing more than to strip off and take a swim.

But since he'd commanded Dione to get dressed he could hardly do that. He closed his eyes instead and called himself all kinds of a fool for allowing such a situation to develop.

Dione took her time getting dressed. What she really wanted to do was walk out of the house and never see Theo again. He was the one to blame. She hadn't invited him to make love to her.

Nor had she stopped him, warned an inner voice.

That was true, but she was damned if she would admit it to him. This was Theo's fault! If he hadn't insisted on this ridiculous marriage then none of it would have happened.

It was with reluctance that she finally made her way outside again. Theo sat with his head back and his eyes closed, but he flicked them open the instant she walked past him. She perched on the edge of the canvas lounger she had vacated earlier, hugged her knees and glared at him.

For a few long seconds neither spoke, resentment pulsing between them like a giant heart. Theo's face was stern, his eyes unwavering, and when she could stand it no longer Dione spoke. 'Where do we go from here?' She knew where she wanted to go; home to England to her mother. Jeannie would take care of her; she would understand why she had been attracted to Theo, and why she needed to get away from him now.

But she couldn't see that happening. There was still a huge chunk of her contract left; Theo wouldn't let her go, especially now she was pregnant with his child.

'First thing, you need to see a doctor; you need confirmation that you are actually pregnant.'

'As if my body hasn't already told me!' she answered quietly, her brown eyes warring with his.

'And, as you seem so reluctant to organise it yourself, while you've been dressing I've made an appointment for you at eleven in the morning with a highly recommended gynaecologist.'

'How dare you?' Dione was incensed that he was taking matters into his own hands. 'You have no right!'

'I have every right, considering that I'm the father,' thrust Theo harshly.

'And then what?' she questioned fiercely. 'Do we

pretend to the world that we're deliriously happy? And what do we do when the contract finishes? Because I sure as hell am not staying with you.'

'We'll cross that bridge when we come to it,' he said with barely concealed anger.

'The coward's way out,' muttered Dione, but he was right, of course. There was very little they could do until the baby arrived. Lord help her if she was going to be tied to Theo because of one simple mistake.

Simple? Not simple! Tortuous perhaps. Stupid! Mindless! Anything but simple! One foolish error was going to affect the rest of her life.

They sat in silence, each deep in their own thoughts, until one of his maids came to tell them that their lunch was ready. It was served indoors, where the air was cool and Dione could breathe more easily, and consisted of a very simple omelette and salad with yoghurt for dessert. Despite her unease in Theo's company, Dione cleaned her plate.

'Are you going back to work?' she asked him, sipping iced water and contemplating the darkness of his brow.

'I'm going to work from home for the rest of the day,' he informed her tersely.

'You don't have to stay with me,' she protested, unable to imagine anything worse under the circumstances. 'I'm not ill; I'll be all right.'

'I'm fully aware of that,' he growled. 'But I intend staying all the same. I think you should rest this afternoon.'

'And what do you think I've been doing all morning?' she asked crossly. 'It's all I ever seem to do.'

'Good.'

'No, it's not good,' she slammed. 'I'm bored witless.'

'I'm sorry you feel that way,' he retorted drily. 'Is there anything you'd rather do?'

Dione hissed her displeasure. She didn't need him to be polite. She would have preferred anger. It was a surreal situation and she hated him for getting her into it.

When she didn't answer he smiled. 'We could go to bed.'

'And do more of the same that got us into this situation in the first place?' she yelled. 'No, thank you! There will be no more sex between us.'

'You can't get pregnant twice.'

Dione eyed him furiously. 'You really have no idea, do you? The very thought of you touching me makes me sick.'

Theo frowned, a deep, harsh frown that dragged his brows together and slashed his forehead. 'You can't mean that.'

'Can't I?' she thrust back.

'It would be impossible. Your body needs mine as much as mine needs yours. Maybe we should put it to the test?' He smiled grimly and walked towards her.

Dione shot to her feet. 'Don't you dare touch me!'

Theo halted mere inches away and to Dione's chagrin her traitorous heart clamoured to break free from her chest, her pulses throbbing in unison to its beat—even her nipples leapt forward in response to his nearness. Every fibre of her being ached for fulfilment! She hated him and wanted him at the same time.

With a groan Theo held out his arms and like a fool she walked into them. He folded her against him and she felt comforting heat as well as scorching awareness.

'It's no use us fighting each other,' he murmured,

nuzzling her ear. 'What's done is done. We might not like it, each for our own reasons, but there's no escaping the fact.'

'You're right,' she agreed, and lifted her mouth for his kiss.

The instant their lips met every sane thought melted away. She was lost yet again in a world where the only things that mattered were their senses. Senses that spiralled away out of control! Touch—the feel of him beneath her fingertips, of a finely honed body, of well-developed muscles, of a barely reined hunger!

'Let's go somewhere we won't be disturbed,' he breathed against her mouth.

Dione nodded her agreement, reluctant to let go, and gave a little squeal of delight when he swung her up into his arms and carried her upstairs.

With his bedroom door kicked shut behind him Theo wasted no time in stripping off his clothes while Dione did the same. They were both consumed by a primeval craving that needed to be urgently assuaged, and as far as Dione was concerned it was a mind-blowing experience, over too quickly, but beautiful all the same.

Did she regret it? She asked herself this frequently in the hours that followed while Theo was working away quietly in his study, and always the answer was the same. No, she did not.

CHAPTER TWELVE

AT PRECISELY eleven o'clock Dione and Theo were ushered into the gynaecologist's consulting room, and at ten minutes past eleven her pregnancy was confirmed. 'Congratulations,' the doctor said to them both.

It wasn't a surprise but even so Dione gazed at Theo in dismay. He took her hand and smiled and tried not to show the doctor that they weren't truly delighted. 'Let's go and celebrate,' he said.

'Mother, I have something to tell you.' Dione's heart was thumping as though she were a guilty sixteen-year-old instead of a married woman in her twenties. And although she hadn't meant to blurt it out quite so immediately she added, 'I'm pregnant.'

She had made a conscious decision not to keep the news from her mother. Jeannie had been hurt enough when she got married without telling her. She didn't deserve to be kept in the dark about her first grandchild.

There was a pause at the other end of the phone, a long pause. 'Do say something,' urged Dione.

'I'm delighted—if you are,' answered Jeannie cautiously.

'I think I'm more shocked,' confessed Dione.

'It is…a little soon in your marriage. How does Theo feel?'

'He's in a state of shock too. But I'm sure that when we've both got used to the idea we'll be over the moon. He's very protective of me; keeps wanting me to rest. I'm sure he thinks I'm ill.'

'Your father was the same,' advised Jeannie. 'Men don't understand these things. When are you expecting it?'

'Next March! Oh, Mother, I wish you were here.'

'You know I can't come over, sweetheart.'

Of course Dione knew. Jeannie would never set foot anywhere near Yannis.

'But you could come home nearer the time and have your baby here,' suggested her mother hesitantly.

'I'd love that,' breathed Dione, 'but I don't think Theo would be too keen on the idea.'

'Of course not,' said Jeannie at once. 'He'll want to be with you. He'll book you into the best maternity hospital and he'll hover over you like a protective butterfly. He loves you very much, Dione.'

It helped that her mother did think Theo was good for her because how could she tell her that the very thought of being tied to him for the rest of her life terrified her? How could she explain her fears that he might snatch the baby from her if she went against his wishes? It would be like a re-run of her mother's torture and she wouldn't wish that on her child for anything. She knew only too well the pain and distress it caused, the nightmares that never completely went away.

She still didn't know whether Theo would expect her to remain married to him permanently. It was something they hadn't yet discussed, and her hormones were too irrational at this moment to even think about it.

They chatted for a while longer and after she'd hung up Dione wandered around the villa like a lost soul. She couldn't drum up any excitement for this new life inside her. Any normal mother would have been making plans and preparations and sharing her excitement with whoever cared to listen.

By the time Theo came home that evening she had worked herself up into such a state that he took one look at her and asked whether she was feeling ill.

'What do you think?' she snapped. 'How would you feel in my position?' She'd been pacing the room, not looking forward to him coming home, wishing herself anywhere but here.

'I think,' he said quietly, taking her shoulders and forcing her to sit down, 'that you should try to relax. I know neither of us is happy with what's happened, but it's done and there's no going back. If you want your baby to be happy and contented then that's what you need to be too.'

'And how would you know?' she demanded with a flash of her lovely dark eyes.

In answer he took the seat beside her, and a deep sadness came over his face. 'There's something I need to tell you.'

Immediately Dione knew what he was going to say and guilt flooded her because she had spoken without thinking.

'Katina and I had a son.'

He didn't look at her as he spoke, for which she was thankful because she didn't want to give away the fact that she already knew.

'Our marriage was a mistake from the start. We never stopped arguing; we each had different aims in life.

Katina's was to play the bored housewife but the perfect partygoer. And that didn't suit my lifestyle. I'm a workaholic, as you've probably gathered, and when I come home I need to relax. Not so Katina. She's a night person. We were totally unsuited and were on the verge of splitting up when she became pregnant.'

Theo's hands were locked between his knees and he rocked ever so slightly backwards and forwards as memories returned. Dione kept as quiet as the proverbial church mouse. This was a side of Theo she hadn't seen before—deeply disturbed and retrospective.

She was almost tempted to put her hand over his but then thought better of it. He was best left alone until he had told her the whole story.

'Katina wasn't too happy at the thought of becoming a mother; she felt it would destroy her hedonistic lifestyle. But I thought it might help save our marriage and was delighted. Nikos was born and for a few months Katina seemed to settle down and be happy. But gradually her desire to party overtook her again.

Theo sprang to his feet and crossed over to the window. The sky had turned purple with faint streaks of scarlet reflected from the sun that had gone down only moments earlier. It was one of the most beautiful and dramatic skies Dione had ever seen. But she knew that Theo was blind to it. In his mind's eye he was seeing only the destruction of his son and his marriage.

Again she wanted to comfort him, but again she knew it was too soon. She waited with bated breath for him to continue.

'One night I was called out to a work-related problem. It was unfortunate that it was Nikos' nanny's night off. Katina had been planning to go out to some friend's birthday bash, and was far from pleased when there was no one to look after Nikos. She didn't trust our housekeeper and so took him with her. All this was without my knowledge, you understand?'

He spun to face her, and Dione drew in a swift breath when she saw the sheer hell in his eyes. But still she remained silent.

'Katina ran her car off the road, braked for a dog or some night animal. She got away with a few scratches and a broken arm, but Nikos was killed.'

Dione drew in a deeply horrified breath, appalled at what she was hearing, and instinctively she jumped up and ran across to Theo. He was blinded by tears and she wrapped her arms around him. 'I'm so sorry, so very sorry,' she said, and there were tears in her eyes too.

For several minutes they stood locked in each other's arms, tears freely flowing, thoughts spinning, until Theo finally pulled away. 'That was seven years ago, and there hasn't been a day gone by when I haven't thought about him.'

'I can understand that,' said Dione softly.

'Katina and I divorced pretty quickly afterwards. She's still single and childless and a proper party animal. We would never have worked. You can see why I was angry that day she came to see you.'

Dione swallowed hard and nodded.

'There have been occasions when she's tried to get back with me, though lord knows why—probably because her money's running out. I settled a pretty hefty sum on her after the divorce and if she's spent it it's her bad luck. She doesn't have a job; she likes to think of herself as a lady of leisure.'

He shook his head as if to clear it of all bad thoughts. 'I'm sorry; I didn't mean to burden you with any of this.'

'I'm glad you've told me,' she said with a quiet smile.

'Nikos would have been seven and a half by now. His birthday's the day before Christmas.' He was speaking more or less to himself, a faint smile curving his lips.

Dione would like to bet that Theo had pictured his son over the years growing into an intelligent young boy, full of mischief and questions, and maybe the very image of his father. It was a dreadful thing to have happened and she couldn't even begin to imagine how she would feel under the same circumstances. Katina had mentioned her son briefly but hadn't shown any signs of grief like Theo, which Dione found truly remarkable.

A long silence followed during which they were both busy with their own thoughts. Then, seeming to throw off the mantle of melancholy that had enveloped him, Theo took Dione gently into his arms. 'How would you like to help me forget for a few hours?'

How could she refuse? With hands linked they went up to their bedroom and then began the sweetest, most tender assault on her senses that Dione had experienced since meeting Theo. She had expected him to be driven, to take her instantly and fiercely in order to fight his inner demons—and she'd been ready for him. Shattering excitement was what their marriage was all about.

Instead he took the utmost satisfaction in undressing her slowly, kissing each inch of bare flesh as it was exposed. Dione had never been treated to such exqui- site pleasures before; had never dreamt that such light kisses could be such torture. She wanted more and she wanted it quickly, but when she reached out to hold him closer he tapped her on the nose.

'Patience, my love,' he said with a soft, mysterious smile.

And so she was forced to stand there until she was completely naked, having suffered the torment of breasts and nipples being sucked into his mouth, of her stomach being smothered with kisses, and as he inched lower and lower so grew her desire.

When finally he knelt before her and his tongue and lips explored and tasted her most private of places, she threw back her head and mewed like a kitten.

She wanted to lie down on the bed She wanted to spread herself wide for him. She wanted him to enter her and make love in such a way that only Theo knew how.

But he was not ready for that yet. He looked up and saw the drugged pleasure in her eyes and with a satisfied smile he pushed himself to his feet. For a second, when he moved away from her, Dione thought that he was going to leave her like that and her whole being screamed out for release.

Instead he said in a voice little more than a hoarse whisper, 'My turn now.'

Dione had never had the pleasure of undressing Theo before; always he'd been so impatient that he tore his clothes off himself. Now, with nervous fingers, she undid the buttons on his shirt, kissing, as he had done, each exposed area of tanned and warm and incredibly potent flesh.

Always, every day, she was aware of the fresh masculine smell of him but never more so than at this moment. As she tasted and touched and inhaled she felt every part of her being sing with excitement. It took an age for her to undo his shirt buttons because her fingers trembled so much.

It was a whole new experience and when finally she slipped it back off his shoulders and the whole of his naked chest was exposed to her greedy eyes she did what he had done to her. She sucked his hard male nipples into her mouth, exulting when she felt his rise of pleasure, when she heard him groan with undisguised anguish, when his fingers gripped her shoulders so hard that they hurt.

She attacked his trousers next, again a totally new experience, and when she had difficulty undoing the waistband he impatiently did it for her. She slid the zip down with deliberate slowness; suddenly beginning to enjoy this game, she enjoyed seeing Theo writhe.

He had tormented her until she'd felt that she was going out of her mind, and now it was her pleasure to do the same to him. She waited until he had stepped out of his trousers and underpants before she touched and kissed and reverently stroked the object of her desire.

Long minutes passed before she tentatively took him into her mouth and if her own desperate need was anything to go by Theo should be almost dying with painful hunger.

When he stopped her, when he groaned and pulled sharply away, Dione knew that he had been on the verge of no return. Neither of them spoke, each aware of the other's need, aware of their own need, and this beautiful, slow seduction of senses.

Their eyes met and by mutual silent consent they fell onto the bed, and here Theo became the master again, entering her slowly, making love slowly, his eyes never leaving hers. Somehow he managed to save himself until he saw the telling reflex in her eyes, when he felt the tensing in her body as she was about to explode, and then, and only then, did he let his own feelings ride free.

Each time they made love was better than the last, but this surpassed everything. Dione thought that she was going to faint as she lay there fighting for breath and crying out Theo's name.

Theo too fought long and hard for control and when finally he moved from her, when he lay on his back, one arm stretched across her, the other hanging over the edge of the bed, she knew what it meant for them both to be truly happy.

Of course, it was going to be an infinitesimal moment in the time span of life, but here, together, there was no future, there was no past, it was just the here and now, and the ultimate release of emotions.

It had been hard telling Dione about Nikos, and he'd hated the fact that he'd broken down in front of her. But now, lying here spent, aware of her gorgeous body next to his, Theo felt his unhappiness over Nikos' death had been put back into that special place in his heart and safely locked away.

How she'd managed to arouse him so erotically, and how he'd hung on so long, he had no idea. Considering Dione had been a virgin when he met her, she had considerable flair. She was like a witch, weaving her magic; knowing instinctively how to turn him on.

And she did it so beautifully. He was lying here spent now but he knew that in a very short space of time he would be ready to start again. He turned his head and smiled lazily at her. She looked radiant, her skin soft and flushed, her lovely dark eyes luminous. 'You're incredible, do you know that?'

Dione gave a Mona Lisa smile, contained and mysterious. 'I did what came naturally.'

He turned onto his side so that he could look at her more easily, smoothing his fingertips over her breasts, feeling the hot moistness of her skin; the rise and fall of breathing that had not yet steadied. 'A natural siren. Aren't I a lucky man?'

Dione remained silent and he guessed that she didn't feel herself so lucky. And who could blame her? He trailed his hand over her stomach, quite flat at this moment, but inside was his baby.

He met her eyes and knew that she was thinking the same and in an instant he had sprung from the bed, guilt settling over him like a devil's cloak. How could he enjoy himself in her body ever again with such a heavy weight to carry?

In the days that followed Theo did his best to keep a distance between himself and Dione, but it was difficult if not impossible. She affected his senses to such an extent that there were times when he could not keep away from her. And she never stopped him when he wanted to make love; in fact, her need was often as strong as his.

It was the only thing they had in common, this hunger for each other's bodies. A crazy situation when looked at in the cold light of day, but a heady one when experienced in the velvet darkness of the night.

He knew that he had a liability towards this child, and he had no intention of shirking it, but he'd been haunted over the years by Nikos' death and, try as he might, he could not shake the thought from his mind that it could happen again to this as yet unborn child. It was an irrational fear, perhaps, but not one he could ignore. He shared his thoughts with no one, not even his mother and father.

'Theo, we've had an invite from your parents.'

'You didn't accept?' He had just come in from an exhausting day at the office and a further meeting with the police. They had indisputable proof now that his exemployee was the hacker, and he'd been charged and was due to appear in front of the magistrate for sentencing in a few days' time.

'I said you'd ring them. They want us to go for dinner on Saturday night.'

Relief showed on his face. 'I thought you meant for tonight, and I couldn't face going out again.' He was mentally weary and wanted nothing more than a peaceful evening at home, perhaps burying himself in Dione's body! It was a pleasure that always made him feel better.

'Dione, it's good to see you again.' Theo's mother, stately in black, her greying hair fixed in a bun at her nape, beamed her pleasure as she led them through to the sheltered garden at the back of their villa. 'I thought we'd sit outside for a while now that some of the heat's gone out of the day.'

It was a much smaller house than Theo's and furnished in a very homely style. Dione felt instantly at ease. A sprinkler kept the lawn green and flowers nodded their lazy heads whenever droplets caught them. It was serene and cool and even Theo stretched out his legs and looked relaxed.

There had been days recently when he looked anything but. Whether it was the court case that bothered him or their own difficult circumstances Dione couldn't be sure. Maybe both! She'd forgotten about the hacker but it had naturally affected Theo and the running of his business affairs. She felt a bit guilty for not asking him how things were.

Theo's father, an older version of Theo himself, poured them drinks and once they were settled his mother looked directly at Dione. 'Tell me how things are going. It's very naughty of Theo not to have brought you to see us before now, but I know how busy he is. It shouldn't stop you coming, though, Dione. You're welcome at any time.'

'Thank you,' she murmured. It was true; apart from a few brief words at the wedding she'd seen nothing of Theo's parents, and he had warned her on their drive over that he hadn't yet told them that she was pregnant. 'Plenty of time for that,' he had said.

In other words, he didn't want her to blurt it out. He needn't have worried; she was doing her very best to forget that she was pregnant. Not that it was easy with morning sickness, but other than that she had never felt better.

'Have you settled into your new home?'

Dione nodded. 'I have; it's very beautiful.'

'I expect your parents are missing you. You did live at home?'

Again Dione inclined her head.

'And I believe your father has been ill. How is he now, poor man? I've eaten at his restaurants. Very good food.'

'He's doing well, thank you. He's over the worst. He's left hospital now.'

'That is good. Give him my best wishes. Theo, he has

not told us very much about you at all. Do you have any brothers or sisters?'

Dione didn't like being given the third degree and she glanced at Theo to see whether he would rescue her. But he was deep in conversation with his father and seemed not to notice. 'I'm an only child,' she answered.

'Such a pity!' consoled the older woman. 'Theo and Alexandra were excellent company for each other. There is only thirteen months between them. Didn't your mother want any more?'

Dione sucked in a breath and answered as evenly as she could, 'Yannis divorced my mother. She lives in England and has never remarried. And my stepmother's never had any children.' And please, she prayed, don't ask me any more personal questions. But it was not to be.

'That is so sad.' Mrs Tsardikos leaned forward and took Dione's hands into hers. 'How old were you when your parents divorced?'

Finally Dione caught Theo's eye and he came to her rescue. 'You ask too many questions, Mother. Why don't you tell Dione about your poetry? I'm sure she'd love to read some.'

Her attention distracted, Mrs Tsardikos released Dione's hands. 'Would you really?' And her pale eyes lit up with pleasure.

Dione nodded. Anything to distract her temporary mother-in-law from this invasion of her privacy!

Smiling happily, the woman hurried indoors.

'You'll have to excuse my wife,' said Theo's father. 'She has a very inquisitive nature. Drink up and I'll pour you another—you'll need it before the night's out. Once Helena gets going there's no stopping her.'

'Dione doesn't drink alcohol,' Theo informed him. 'I'm sorry, I forgot to tell you.'

'Dear me,' muttered the older man. 'And here was I, thinking she did not like it. So what would you like? Fruit juice? Mineral water?'

'Just water, please,' answered Dione, and when Theo's father disappeared too she looked at Theo crossly. 'Why didn't you warn me about your mother? I think she wants to know my whole family history.'

Theo grinned. 'She's just curious, that's all. There's no harm in her. But poetry's her pet hobby so you'll be asked no more questions, except perhaps whether you like it or not. I have to admit it's not to my taste.'

'And what if it's not to mine? Do I tell her?'

Theo shrugged and spread his hands. 'That's up to you.'

In other words, on her head be it.

But Dione got through the next half-hour quite happily. Fortunately she liked Helena's poetry: it was rich and thought-provoking; all about life. And it was easier to see now why she asked such a lot of questions. She knew so much about people, what made them act the way they did, their sorrows and happiness, their beliefs and opinions.

'Have you ever thought about getting them pub-lished?' she asked. They were written in a hard-backed book in the most beautiful handwriting and Dione could just see them in print, with perhaps telling illustrations beside each one.

'Nonsense, child; they're not good enough for that. I think it's time we had dinner. Let's go indoors.' And her poetry was dismissed.

It was a long, leisurely meal with an assortment of both meat and fish dishes that left the tastebuds bursting. After dessert, an out-of-this-world strawberry flan, Theo's father suggested they take their coffee outside. He loved his garden and was never happier than when he was working in it or talking about it.

When Dione made to follow Helena placed a hand on her arm and held her back until the men were out of earshot. 'There's something I must ask you, child. Why have you not told me that you're pregnant?'

CHAPTER THIRTEEN

DIONE'S eyes snapped wide and her heart ran amok. How had Helena found out about the baby? Had Theo told her after all?

'It's all right, child, Theo hasn't said anything,' reassured her mother-in-law, reading her thoughts. 'But I'm a woman; I know these things. It should be a happy time for you, but Theo, he is not so happy?'

Dione's fine brows drew together. How had his mother guessed? Surely she didn't know the circumstances of their marriage? Her face suddenly went bright red. If Theo had told her she would...

'I'm right, aren't I?' interjected the older woman quickly. 'He's not happy. And I will tell you why. It is because of little Nikos. My son, he doesn't say much to me; in fact, he doesn't speak about it at all, much to my sadness. But it broke his heart when Nikos died.' And then she clapped a hand to her mouth, her pale eyes suddenly horrified. 'You do know about him?'

'Yes, Theo told me,' acknowledged Dione with a nod.

A look of relief crossed Helena's face. 'He would never forgive me if I said something out of place. You see, I truly thought my Theo would have no more children. He idolised that boy and no one can ever replace him.' She lifted her hands and shook them in the air in desperation. 'I think he is wrong; I think this child you are carrying will be good for him. But you must be patient, Dione, if he does not at first seem happy.'

If only she knew the real reason for Theo's displeasure, thought Dione, but she smiled wanly. 'I'm sure you're right.'

'I'm glad we have had this talk,' said Helena. 'It will be our little secret for a while, until Theo himself sees fit to tell me.'

When they joined the men Theo looked at Dione with a questioning lift of a brow, but she smiled and began chatting normally as though nothing out of the ordinary had happened. A few minutes later Alexandra turned up. Her mother berated her daughter for not saying she was coming. 'You could have joined us for dinner.'

But Theo's sister shrugged it off. 'I didn't know you were having a party.'

And not long afterwards Theo announced that it was time for them to leave.

'Come again, Dione, any time,' said his mother, hugging her warmly. 'Don't wait for Theo to bring you.'

On their way home Theo asked her what his mother had been talking about after dinner. 'I saw her detain you.'

'Nothing much,' insisted Dione, not wishing to break his mother's confidence.

'I want to know,' he declared fiercely. 'I want no secrets.'

Dione sighed and knew that she'd get no peace until she had told him. 'Ok, but you're not to tell her that you know. She guessed about the baby.'

'What?' Disbelief flooded his face. 'How?'

Dione lifted her shoulders. 'Female intuition, I guess.'

'Damn!'

'Does it really matter?' she questioned. 'As soon as I begin to show it will be common knowledge.'

'I wished to choose my own time,' he answered. 'And it certainly wasn't now.'

Dione wasn't sure why but one look at his thunderous face and she knew she dared not ask.

Depending on his mood of the day Dione sometimes slept in her own bed, sometimes in Theo's. Tonight, when they got home, she went straight to her own room. She had no idea why the fact that his mother knew about the baby should upset him so much. Admittedly he didn't want this child, but the deed was done, there was no going back, so why keep it a big secret?

She woke on Sunday morning and Theo's housekeeper told her that he was out, presumably gone to his office, and that he'd left even before she had arisen.

It was something he did occasionally—his mother had told her that it had been a regular thing after his divorce. And now he was unhappy again and wanted to immerse himself in work! Was that it? Not that it was her fault his mother had found out. If he was mad with anyone it should have been his parent.

By mid-morning Dione was feeling well enough to work up an anger against him, and on an impulse she asked his driver to take her to his office. Theo had made sure from the outset that there was always a car and driver at her disposal. The fact that she had her own car seemed not to matter to him, and it sat idly in the garage, probably dying a silent death, wondering why on earth she had abandoned it.

Maybe she was wrong, maybe he had a lot to do, but for once she didn't feel like sitting at home twiddling her thumbs. This marriage had been Theo's idea and he couldn't shirk his responsibilities when something happened that he didn't like.

The office block was in the centre of Athens' business quarter, a magnificent marble building that told the world that this was a truly successful company. Heavy plate-glass doors and a thickset man in uniform guarded its entrance.

'I've come to see my husband,' Dione told him when he looked at her with suspicion. 'Mr Theo Tsardikos.'

The man frowned. 'Mr Tsardikos isn't in today.'

'Yes, he is,' insisted Dione.

'I've not seen him. Just one moment.' And he spoke into an internal phone. 'No, he's not here. I'm sorry if you've had a wasted journey, Mrs Tsardikos.' And then he smiled for the first time. 'I'm pleased to meet you. I've heard talk about the new Mrs Tsardikos. You're even more beautiful than people say.'

'Thank you,' she acknowledged, but too annoyed with Theo to be really pleased. 'Is there anywhere else he's likely to be? I know it's business that called him away.'

'You could try the hotel. He's sometimes there on a Sunday.'

The Tsardikos was one of Athens' premium hotels; royalty and the insanely rich stayed there and Dione had never even put a foot inside the place before. Now, as her driver dropped her off, she craned her neck to look at the towering building. Impressive didn't even begin to describe it and she felt distinctly overwhelmed as she was ushered inside.

It was all marble and mirrors and silent-footed staff and before she'd even reached the reception desk Dione caught sight of Theo coming down a flight of stairs with a stunning redhead on his arm. They were laughing into each other's face and looked completely at ease with one another.

Her stomach bunched into a tight knot and she felt sick; not with her morning sickness but something entirely different. Jealousy! In that instant it hit her. She was beginning to fall in love with Theo!

The shocking discovery stuck in her throat like a fishbone. This was the last thing she had expected or even wanted. Considering their marriage was nothing more than a sham, Theo was free to see other women. Wasn't he? It was amazing how much the thought hurt.

She walked across to him and the shock on his face was something that would stay with her for a long time.

'Dione!' he exclaimed, hurrying forward. 'Is something wrong?'

'No,' she answered as pleasantly as she was able under the circumstances. 'I needed to get out, that's all.'

To her surprise he looked pleased. 'I'm glad you did. Let me introduce you to Belinda, my PA.'

Belinda stepped forward and held out her hand. 'You're Theo's wife? I'm pleased to meet you at last.'

Her handshake was warm and her eyes were friendly but Dione held back. 'I didn't realise that he got you working on a Sunday as well.'

'I work whenever Theo wants me,' answered the redhead, with a warm smile in Theo's direction.

'Belinda's been with me for many years,' Theo informed her. 'She's half-English, like yourself, and I don't know what I'd do without her.'

'Lucky you,' said Dione, managing a faint smile. 'How did you know where to find me?'

'Your office doorman,' she answered. 'He obviously knows your movements better than I do.'

'Well, my work here's finished,' Theo declared. 'Belinda and I were both about to head home. Come, let us go,' and he put a hand beneath her elbow. 'I'll see you in the morning, Belinda.'

Once she had gone his grip on Dione's arm tightened. 'What do you hope to achieve by chasing after me like this?'

'I wasn't chasing,' she answered evenly. 'I was just fed up of being on my own. I'm sorry if I intruded.'

His eyes went rock-hard. 'I don't know what you're talking about.'

'It doesn't matter,' Dione answered quietly.

Theo's lips compressed until they were no more than a thin straight line. 'Am I right in thinking that you suspect there's something going on between Belinda and me?'

'Of course not!' But even to her own ears her words didn't ring true.

'You're wrong, you know. It's your hormones all out of kilter.'

'There's nothing wrong with my hormones,' she said evenly, not wanting to argue with Theo. She knew what she had seen and now all she wanted to do was go home.

'Believe me, I know. It is your hormones,' he rasped.

And he should know because he'd gone through it all before. That was what she expected him to tell her but he didn't. He dismissed Dione's car and driver and jumped into his own, which had glided to a halt outside the doors the instant he set his foot out.

But Dione didn't marvel at the slick organisation, she was too upset, too hurt by her own startling discovery. How it could have happened she had no idea. Falling in love with a man like Theo was a fatal mistake.

When they arrived home the first thing Theo did was pour himself a drink, the second was to stand staring out of the window while he presumably got his thoughts into some sort of order, and the third was to tower over Dione where she had slumped into an easy chair.

'So you think I'm having an affair?' Harsh, condemning lines scored his face and hardened his eyes. 'You think that I'm carrying on with my PA?' The words slammed into her like bullets from a gun. 'Do you really believe that I'd do such a thing while I'm married to you?'

'Ours isn't a proper marriage,' she reminded him quietly. 'You're free to carry on as many affairs as you like.' It hurt to say that but it was the truth whether she liked it or not.

'Even so,' he answered, 'I have principles. And more especially since you're carrying my baby.'

'*Your* baby!' queried Dione. 'I hope you're not trying to say that I'll have no part to play in bringing the child up?' She had thought about this over and over again, but hadn't actually made a decision—until now! She couldn't afford to risk that at some time in their future he would take their child from her. She needed it to be sorted from the very beginning.

In answer Theo took her by the shoulders and would have shaken her, she felt sure, if he hadn't had second thoughts about her condition. 'I'll ignore that remark, Dione, put it down to your hormonal changes.'

'What is it with you and hormones?' she asked. 'It was your hormones that got us into this mess in the first place.'

Their eyes met and held and Dione refused to back down so it was Theo who eventually moved. His fingers curled into his palms, his huge body taut as he stood looking down at her, and his eyes were so hard and black that they looked like time bombs about to explode.

Impatiently he swung away and picked up his glass, tossing the contents down his throat before crossing the room and pouring another, which went exactly the same way.

'I have no wish to argue with you, Dione,' he announced tersely.

'Nor do I,' she answered. 'Does Belinda know about the circumstances of our marriage?'

Theo's top lip curled in a snarl. 'What the hell do you take me for?'

There was something dangerously exciting about Theo in this mood and Dione shifted uncomfortably. 'I've not known you long enough to know what you're really like.' Except that he was beginning to get beneath her skin far more devastatingly than she had expected or even wanted.

'I have not told Belinda, I have not told anyone,' he announced harshly, 'and I hope the same can be said for you.'

'Naturally.'

He swung away again, his rage ebbing and flowing like the ocean that lapped down below them. 'This conversation is getting us nowhere, Dione. I'm going for a swim before lunch.' And with that he marched out of the room.

Dione exhaled slowly and closed her eyes. The morning's ordeal had taken a lot out of her. She felt drained of all energy and emotions. It would be comforting to have Theo's arms around her but she knew that she dared not sleep with him any more, or even let him kiss her, otherwise she would be in great danger of giving herself away.

She picked at her lunch and then, declaring that she was tired, took herself to her room and lay down. Theo did not come after her. She had half expected him to but was not entirely surprised that he didn't. The atmosphere over lunch, which Anna had set out in the shade by the pool, had been thick enough to cut with a knife.

Later, after her scanty meal had gone down, Dione felt it was her turn to swim. She used the pool often when Theo was at work but not very often did they swim together. Now she swam long, lazy lengths alone, the water silken and cool against her skin, and gradually some of the tension eased out of her.

Until suddenly she became aware of someone swimming at her side! She tried to ignore him but Theo was a larger-than-life person and could not be easily dismissed. 'Are you feeling better?' he asked as they reached the end and paused a moment before embarking on another length.

'I'm OK,' she acknowledged softly.

And that was the full length of their conversation. They simply swam up and down the pool, never hurrying, Theo keeping pace with her. The sun blazed down out of a cloudless sky but the water remained mercifully cool and when she'd finally had enough and hauled herself out Theo continued to swim.

Dione watched until her eyes grew heavy and she fell asleep. The next thing she knew Theo was sitting on a chair next to her, watching her through narrowed lids, and she grew uncomfortably warm, wondering how long he had been there.

And suddenly, as she looked down at herself, Dione realised that her stomach was no longer as flat as it had been. It wasn't rounded, but usually when she lay on her back it was hollow—and now it wasn't.

And it was this part of her that Theo was looking at.

With her clothes on it was indiscernible and she hadn't really been aware of it herself—until she followed Theo's gaze. Even her breasts seemed bigger and she grew hot again at the thought of what was happening to her body.

When he realised she was awake Theo got abruptly to his feet. On a table was a jug of iced water and a plate of biscuits. 'You ate hardly anything at lunch time,' he said, filling a glass and handing it to her.

But although Dione drank the water she declined a biscuit. 'I'm not hungry.'

'Even after all that swimming?'

'Yes.'

'It's not good for you to miss your meals. You have two to think about now.'

As if she didn't know it. Unconsciously Dione put her hand on her stomach.

'And this little fellow,' said Theo, placing his hands over hers, 'needs all the nourishment he can get.'

Having him touch her like this was very personal and Dione shifted uneasily. Theo in a bad mood she could handle, but in the light of her new-found feelings it was a different matter altogether.

She moved his hand away. 'Please don't touch me like that.' And she ignored the fact that little quivers of pleasure had begun to run through her.

Dark brows rose. 'You're still annoyed with me?'

'I have no feelings one way or the other,' she told him with an insouciant lift of her shoulders.

Theo frowned. 'In that case it might be best if I left you alone. Do as you like, Dione. Think what you like. But bear in mind that our contract isn't over yet.' With that he spun on his heel and headed indoors.

And the next morning his anger hadn't abated. He came into her room before she had got up, dressed in his suit, ready to go out. And the heavy lines on his face told her that he wasn't here to ask how she was.

'I have to go to Canada on a business trip,' he announced abruptly. 'And I don't know when I'll be back.'

CHAPTER FOURTEEN

DIONE stared at Theo as though he had just told her that he was going to jump off the edge of the planet.

'Don't worry; you'll be well looked after. And probably a whole lot happier with me out of the way,' he added harshly.

Maybe, maybe not! She didn't fancy being cooped up here in this fancy house with no one to talk to. Without a doubt she was going to miss him.

'And don't even think about leaving,' he added shortly when he saw the mixed emotions on her face. 'You're mine—don't ever forget it.'

If they hadn't had their argument yesterday Dione wondered whether he would have asked her to accompany him. She would have liked that. Canada was a place she had often thought she'd like to visit. Vancouver. Ontario. The Niagara Falls. But clearly he didn't want her with him.

Was he taking Belinda? she wondered as he turned and left the room. Would he have someone to keep him warm in bed at night? The very thought sent a stream of jealousy through her stomach. She would be lying here alone and he would be…

Later that morning Dione phoned her mother. 'Theo's gone away for a few days,' she told her. She was missing him already. Not that he was ever around during the day, but she'd got used to him coming home at night and they would sit and talk about all and sundry, sometimes his work, sometimes world affairs, sometimes his parents. They were usually comfortable in each other's company.

And of course often they made love. They had been the best times of all. This was what she was going to miss. She had to accept the fact that she was not the only woman in his life.

His marriage to her was nothing more than a convenient arrangement and she ought to be used to the idea. If it hadn't been for the life growing inside her she might have been. One unfortunate mistake had ruined everything. Actually, two mistakes. The second was discovering she had feelings for him.

'And it's business and he couldn't take you with him,' said her mother, understanding the situation instantly. 'Why don't you come home? I'd love to see you again.'

'I'd like to do that, Mother, but I feel my place is here. I'm settled now; I'm quite happy.'

'Of course you are. Is everything all right with the baby?'

'Perfect.'

'How's Yannis?'

'He's good; he's out of hospital.'

They spoke a few minutes more, and then Dione let her mother go. She supposed she ought to visit her father. Speaking about him had made her feel guilty. She didn't go as often as she ought these days. Even so, she had no intention of telling him about the baby. Yannis would be delighted; he would see it as a way of cementing their relationship permanently.

You can't do better than to marry a nice Greek man! His words haunted her; it had been his mantra ever since she was of marriageable age. Dione shook her head in despair. She would leave it until another day to pay him a visit. In the mood she was in now she might say something she'd be sorry for.

But the next day she regretted that she hadn't been to see him.

'Dione!' It was Phrosini's urgent voice on the phone. 'Your father's in hospital again. He's had another heart attack.'

Dione drew in a swift breath, her heart dipping. 'I'll be right there.'

When she got to the hospital they wouldn't let her see her father. Phrosini was outside his room, wringing her hands, and when she saw Dione she burst into tears. Dione hugged her stepmother and tried to console her. 'He'll be all right, you'll see. My father's a fighter if nothing else.'

But two hours later Yannis died.

Phrosini was beside herself and Dione was upset as well. No matter what she had thought about Yannis, he was her father, her own flesh and blood; he had created her the same as Theo had created the life form inside her own body. There was a bond that nothing could break; not hatred, not anger, not resentment. Nothing!

They sat in an ante-room consoling each other, and it was a long time before either of them felt strong enough to go home. It was sad to think that Yannis would never again be a part of their lives.

'Come home with me,' urged Phrosini. 'I can't be on my own right now.'

From there Dione rang her mother and Jeannie was truly shocked when she heard the news. 'I thought he was getting better?'

'So did I. I guess he's been under more strain than any of us realised.' And at least her mother was free of him now. She might not have seen him for almost twenty years but she'd always remained afraid of him; had never wanted to do anything that might rock the boat and keep her from seeing her darling Dione ever again.

'And how are you, Dione? This isn't going to be too much for you, in your condition?'

'I'm pregnant, Mother, not ill,' she answered, trying to inject a touch of humour into her voice. Not easy at a time like this.

'You will let me know when the funeral is? I'd like to send some flowers.'

'Of course,' answered Dione. 'Will you be OK, Mother?' For the first time she wanted her mother to have company.

'I'll be fine, Dione, don't worry,' Jeannie informed her. 'If you're thinking I shouldn't be on my own then don't. I'll be all right.'

Next it was Theo's turn to be told the news and because she didn't know where he was staying Dione rang his office and was put through to Belinda. Which surprised her, as she'd half thought that his PA might have gone with him on his North American trip.

'Belinda,' she said without preamble, 'I need to get in touch with Theo and he forgot to leave me his hotel number.'

'Are you all right, Dione?' asked the redhead, concern in her voice. 'You sound upset.'

'I just want his number,' said Dione, not wishing to talk about her father's death.

'One moment.' Belinda's voice became efficient and as soon as she had the information she wanted Dione rang off.

It was several hours before she was able to get in touch with Theo. She could have rung his cellphone but she didn't have his number with her. But Dione knew that it wasn't that urgent. Theo didn't give a damn about her father. He would probably think it a good thing that he'd gone.

And then another thought struck her.

Unless Phrosini carried on Yannis' business it would be sold. Theo could have his money back. She would be free of him!

Amazingly the thought saddened her. In fact she felt quite tearful. She didn't want to be free of Theo, not any more. She wanted him to love her the way she was beginning to love him. Not that there was any chance of that.

'Dione, what's wrong? Belinda told me you'd be calling.'

Dione didn't appreciate the fact that the redhead had felt fit to inform him that his wife had been after his hotel number.

'She said you sounded upset. Are you ill? It's not the baby, is it?' he asked with sudden concern in his voice.

'As if you'd care,' she thrust with a sudden gush of anger. 'It would be a relief for you if I lost it, wouldn't it?' And then she wished she hadn't said that. It was cruel and unnecessary and she didn't really mean it.

There was a long silence at the other end and Dione knew that he was hanging on to his temper by a thin thread.

'I'm sorry,' she said. 'That was uncalled for.'

'So why did you want to speak to me?' His voice was hard and entirely devoid of emotion and Dione could see in her mind's eye the harsh planes of his face.

'It's my father,' she announced in a voice scarcely above a whisper now. 'He—he had another heart attack. He died this morning.' And telling Theo like this made it a stone-cold fact.

Up until now she had not really taken in the fact that Yannis was no longer with them. It would leave a great big hole in her life, in all the lives of those he had touched—especially Phrosini, who had loved him unconditionally. And who even now had shut herself in her room. She had cried until she could cry no more. Whereas Dione had not shed a single tear!

She didn't feel guilty. She was sorry her father had died, of course she was, but he had hurt her so much over the years that tears refused to come.

'Dione! I'm so sorry,' said Theo, his voice reverent and hushed now.

But she knew that he wasn't. He'd had no time for Yannis and hadn't been afraid to show it.

'Is there anything I can do?'

'No,' she said quickly and firmly. 'Phrosini and I will take care of things. I'm with her now. I'm staying here until after the funeral.'

'Of course! I'll come home as soon as I possibly can.' And after a slight pause, 'Dione—'

'Yes?'

'Are you all right? Really all right, I mean? In your condition it's—'

And that was all he cared about, her condition. 'I'm fine,' she said quietly. 'I don't need wrapping in cotton wool, Theo.' And she put down the phone.

Almost immediately she wished that she hadn't. She had heard the concern in his voice; he could be a great source of comfort to her—if she gave him the chance! She dropped her head in her hands. What was happening to her? Why was she behaving so badly?

Theo claimed it was her hormones. Perhaps he was right. Or perhaps it was because she was falling in love with him and dared not let him see it.

'Mother! What are you doing here?' It was the morning of the funeral and a taxi had just dropped Jeannie off at Dione's father's house. A surprisingly confident Jeannie with a different hairstyle and new clothes.

'I thought you might need me, my darling,' answered her mother. 'You don't think Phrosini will mind?'

'Of course not,' said Dione at once, but Phrosini had never met Jeannie and Dione couldn't be truly sure what her reaction would be. There had been no consoling her since her husband's death. Dione herself had had to make all the arrangements, and Phrosini was even at this very moment shut in a darkened room. Crying tears for her beloved Yannis when Dione had thought she could not possibly cry any more. 'I'll tell her you're here.'

Phrosini at once took Jeannie into her arms and both women cried.

'Where's Theo?' asked Jeannie finally.

'Still in Canada,' answered Dione quietly and sadly. 'He said he'd try to get away, but—'

'And he did,' said a deep voice over her shoulder.

Dione felt the hairs on the back of her neck prickle and she spun around. Theo, in a black suit and tie, stood sombrely in front of her. 'Theo—you didn't tell me you were coming today.'

It was a flat statement of fact, yet inside her, despite the ordeal that lay ahead, she felt her body react to Theo's innate sexuality in a way that it shouldn't on a day like this. Or on any other day for that matter!

'You didn't really think I would stay away?' asked Theo shortly once they were alone. 'Keristari might not have been my favourite person, but he was your father and I respect that. I'm here for you, Dione. It can't have been easy arranging the funeral; if I could have got away earlier I would have, but—'

'I don't need you,' Dione told him coolly. 'My mother's here for me.'

'Not for Yannis?'

'What do you think after the way he treated her? My mother's a different person these days. She made the journey alone and I really admire her for that.'

Theo couldn't even begin to describe the feelings that ate at his gut. At first, when Dione had appeared to be jealous of Belinda he'd felt surprisingly pleased, but now that she still showed no sign of even liking him he was at odds to know what his emotions were.

Yannis dying put a whole new complexion on things. Strictly speaking there was no reason now for Dione to remain tied to him. She had probably worked this out for herself! But in truth he didn't want to let her go. She was carrying his baby! And, although he was deeply fearful of bringing another child into the world, it didn't alter the way he felt about Dione.

Dione had grown on him in a way he hadn't expected. He got angry with her sometimes, deeply angry, but in many other ways she was a delight in his life. Spending time away had helped him get things into perspective, but to return home and find Dione still very much out of favour with him was like someone driving a stake into his heart.

After the funeral, with only Phrosini and Jeannie and Dione left, Theo took Dione to one side and asked her what she wanted to do. 'Are you coming home?' he asked gently.

Dione appeared to consider his suggestion, and then shook her head. 'Phrosini still needs me.'

He felt his temper begin to rise. 'Phrosini has your mother now.' He hoped it didn't show in his voice. This was no place for an argument. 'She's not leaving until tomorrow—I asked her. They've discovered a strange alliance. In fact I think Jeannie might stay even longer.'

'Do you know,' asked Dione, 'that this is the first time she's visited Greece?'

Theo inclined his head. 'She told me so. I imagine she's feeling relief. And I don't mean that in a nasty way, Dione,' he added when he saw her lips tighten. 'Yannis was her nemesis.'

'I know,' agreed Dione reluctantly. 'And I'm happy she's here.'

'So you will come home?'

'I'm not sure, Theo.'

Exasperated, Theo saw red. 'You will come, Dione. Your place is with me now.' He hadn't wanted to come down the high and mighty, but she was driving him insane. All the time he'd been in Canada he had wanted her in his bed. She had no idea how empty his hotel room had been.

He watched as Dione struggled with her emotions. She was so beautiful; he had almost forgotten how beautiful. He had never seen her in black before, except for her bikini, which didn't count. No, that was wrong. It did count. He adored seeing her long golden limbs and her amazingly slender body. Which was already changing shape!

Pregnancy suited her, gave her a glow that had been absent before—except perhaps when they made love! She looked stunning now, though. Elegant, almost regal as she stood in front of him with her chin held high and her gorgeous dark eyes blazing.

'Very well, I'll come,' she answered quietly, almost submissively. Which wasn't the usual Dione style, and he hated himself for pressurising her on today of all days. He knew he was being cruel but the truth was he needed her

But when they got home it didn't turn out as he'd hoped. Almost before they'd set foot through the door she turned on him. 'Don't think we can pick up where we left off, Theo. It's the last thing I want to do.'

'Of course,' he answered as evenly as he could. 'It's been a horrible day for you. All I want to do is hold and comfort you, to let you know that—' he had been about to say that he'd always be at her side. Where had that idea come from? Dione was showing him in no uncertain terms that he would never be a permanent fixture in her life '—that I care.'

'Care?' she echoed. 'I bet you didn't even think about me while you were in Canada. You probably even had female company. And then of course you have Belinda waiting for you when your wife turns you out of her bed.'

'In fact,' Dione went on before he could say anything, 'I can't think why I let you persuade me to come home. You and I no longer have anything in common. I'm not staying. I'm going back to my fa—to Phrosini's.' And so saying she spun on her heel and rushed out of the house.

For a few moments Theo didn't follow; he simply stood there in a state of shock. He hadn't expected her to flare up like this. Both the funeral and her pregnancy must be playing havoc with her nerves.

He must go after her, calm her down, make her see that he only had her best interests at heart. But before he could even do that he heard a cry and a crash—and the next moment silence!

CHAPTER FIFTEEN

THEO raced to the front door, his heartbeats quick and hard, coming to a shocked halt when he saw Dione lying motionless at the bottom of the steps that led on to the driveway. Instantly he was kneeling at her side, calling her name, not attempting to move her in case she had broken something.

When she didn't respond he yanked his cellphone out of his pocket and called for an ambulance. 'Quickly!' he barked. 'My wife's knocked herself out and she's pregnant.' And all the time his eyes were on her.

She was breathing, thank goodness, but there was a nasty cut on her forehead that was oozing blood. He stemmed it with his handkerchief and held it there until Dione stirred and lifted heavy lids to look at him. 'What—?'

'Shh!' He pressed a finger to her lips. 'Don't say anything; don't even try to move. There's an ambulance on its way.'

'I don't want—'

'Just a precaution,' he told her. 'Hopefully they'll send you home, but you need to be checked over. That was some fall you took.'

Dione closed her eyes and lay so still that he was fearful she'd passed out again.

'Theo!' It was no more than a husky whisper.

He bent forward and put his ear close to her lips. 'Yes?'

'Do you think I've harmed the baby?'

'Of course not,' he said reassuringly, though his thoughts had already run along similar lines. What if he lost this child the way he had lost Nikos? It didn't bear thinking about; it would be his biggest nightmare come true. He shivered, his body ice-cold, and it seemed an age before the ambulance arrived.

When it did he went with Dione and walked alongside the trolley as she was wheeled to the emergency room. But he was not permitted to stay while she was examined, and he paced the corridor like a caged animal.

It seemed an age before someone finally came to tell him that she would be all right. 'She's bruised her head badly and has a severe headache, and we're keeping her in for a few days just to make sure.'

'Is that necessary?' asked Theo with a sharp frown. 'If it's just her head then—'

'She *is* pregnant, Mr Tsardikos,' reminded the doctor. 'A fall like this could cause a miscarriage. She needs to rest. And I'm sure she wouldn't do that at home.'

'No, I expect you're right,' agreed Theo, but even so he wasn't happy. She'd just buried her father, for goodness' sake; she'd had enough of hospitals. 'I could look after her myself,' he said. 'Make sure she rests.'

'No, Mr Tsardikos.' The doctor held up her hand. 'She stays here. You can obviously visit whenever you like, even stay here if you prefer; there will be a room next to your wife's for family.'

'I'll stay,' agreed Theo at once. 'I'll go home and get some clothes and be back before you know it. Can I tell Dione?'

'I'm sorry, she really does need to rest.'

In the hours that followed Theo watched Dione as she slept, knowing that it was his fault she was here. If he hadn't insisted on her accompanying him home they would never have argued and this wouldn't have happened. Hell, why could he never control his temper? Dione had grown on him more than he'd ever expected and he knew that he was already halfway to falling in love with her. If anything should happen…

Finally, though, he fell into a fitful sleep and the next thing he knew she was calling his name.

'Dione!' he breathed thankfully. 'You're awake at last. How are you feeling?' She looked pale and lifeless and he was dreadfully worried.

'I want my mother.'

It was like a blow to his solar plexus. Nevertheless he didn't show that it hurt. He glanced at the clock on the wall instead. 'It's the middle of the night,' he said gently.

'I still want her.'

'Won't I do? Is there something you need?' he asked. 'I'm sure that—'

'Theo,' she insisted, 'I need my mother.' She said it very firmly and very loudly and her eyes were hard on his, telling him without words that she didn't want him sitting watching her.

'Very well,' he said on a sigh and with great reluctance. 'I'll go and fetch her.' He supposed it was natural that at a time like this she would want her mother. But it hurt that she was turning to someone else instead of him. He should be the one uppermost in her mind; he was her husband after all.

But in what way? asked an inner voice. Your marriage is nothing more than a sham. Dione doesn't love you; it was out of loyalty to her father that she married you. You'd best remember that.

He didn't want to remember, damn it. Dione meant a lot to him now and he wanted to look after her the same as any husband would.

When he arrived at her father's house it took a long while for him to make anyone hear, and when the door was finally opened it was Jeannie herself who stood there.

'Theo?' Her eyes widened with surprise. 'Is something wrong?'

He didn't waste time with apologies. 'Dione's had a fall…she's in hospital; she's asking for you. Get yourself dressed and I'll take you right now.'

Jeannie's face blanched. 'She is all right?'

He nodded.

'And the baby?'

'So far everything seems fine.'

'What do you mean?' she asked with a further frown.

'Apparently there's danger of a miscarriage, so she has to rest. They're keeping her in for a few days.'

'Thank goodness I'm here,' breathed Jeannie as she turned away. Belatedly she said, 'You'd better come in. I'll leave Phrosini a note. I don't want to wake her; she had trouble getting to sleep.'

But while Theo was waiting Phrosini herself came to see what was going on and Theo explained all over again what had happened. 'I'll keep you posted,' he said. 'I'm so sorry, Phrosini.'

But all was well and after three days Dione was allowed home and Jeannie reluctantly flew back to England. She had wanted to stay and help look after her daughter but Theo had persuaded her otherwise. He wanted to take care of Dione himself; he wanted to show her in every way possible how much he cared.

'You gave me a big scare,' said Theo once he'd settled Dione in a comfortable chair.

'I scared myself,' she admitted with a wry smile.

'But you are OK now?' She still looked pale and tired and he couldn't help worrying.

Dione nodded.

Theo sat down close to her and leaned forward. He wanted to take her hands and blurt out the fact that he had fallen in love with her, but he knew that he dared not. Not yet, at least. 'I have something to tell you,' he said, his heart thumping as painfully as if he were a teenager on his first date. He hadn't felt like this in a long time.

Dione looked at him expectantly.

'I never really wanted this baby of ours,' he began.

'I know that,' she retorted quickly.

'No, hear me out,' he insisted, 'I've not finished. I've always been afraid that I'd lose him the same as I did Nikos. Life is such a precarious thing. I couldn't have handled it. I'd rather have no children than fear losing another. At least that's what I thought.'

He had her full attention now and he swallowed hard before continuing. 'But when the nurse told me there could be a danger of you miscarrying I knew that if that happened I'd want to kill myself. I love that little life growing inside you. The same as I've grown to love you, Dione.' He twisted his lips wryly and looked at her with his heart in his eyes. 'Do you think you could ever learn to love me in return?'

He watched as Dione's eyes grew wide and round and then she turned her head away and he knew that he had lost her.

Theo's admittance didn't altogether surprise Dione. His vigil at her bedside had proved how much he cared. And even though she'd been afraid to let herself believe it she had felt his love radiating out to her.

Nevertheless she remained silent.

'You think I don't mean it?' he asked harshly. 'You're surely not still thinking that there's something going on between Belinda and me?'

'You looked so close,' she answered miserably.

Theo closed his eyes for a brief second and took a breath. 'Belinda has a boyfriend; they're getting engaged at Christmas. She's extremely happy. She's been with me for a long time and admittedly we have a strong rapport that is sometimes misread. But believe me she means nothing to me in the way you think.'

He turned her to face him, his hands hot on her shoulders, searing her skin, making her want to lean into him and feel his strong arms around her. 'And that's all there is to it.'

Dione gave a small sigh. 'I know there's nothing going on between you, really I do. I'm sorry for doubt-ing you.' But there was still something else troubling her. 'Would you love me if I wasn't pregnant, Theo?' she asked in low, hushed tones. She needed to be absolutely sure that his declaration of love wasn't simply for the baby's sake.

'Dione, I think I fell in love with you the day you

came to see me on your father's behalf,' answered Theo with a smile. 'You were unlike anyone else I'd ever met. You intrigued me and I knew I had to make you mine.'

'So you thought up that heinous plot?' she challenged, her eyes growing softer, but still she didn't let their bodies touch. She was teasing him now, wanting to see how long it was before he could contain himself no longer.

'You have to admit that it was a pretty good one.'

'So what happens now my father's died?' she challenged.

'The contract still stands,' he declared firmly. 'In fact, I'm thinking of increasing it to life. Could you bear that, Dione?'

In response she lifted her mouth to his, at the same time pressing the full length of her body against him. His arousal was swift and exciting, sending fresh waves of sensation through every inch of her being. The kiss, gentle at first, increased in passion with each second that passed, until finally Theo swung her into his arms and carried her up to bed.

'One thing, *agapi mou*, before I ravish you sense-less,' he growled, his fingers trailing sensual delights over her already naked body. 'I haven't heard you say yet that you love me.'

'Isn't it obvious?' she asked, her tone so husky that he had to bend his head to hear. Lying in her hospital bed, wondering whether she was going to lose her baby, had made her realise how precious life was, and how short. There wasn't time for arguments, for hiding feelings. It was the here and now that mattered.

'I love you, Theo.' And she rather liked the sound of it. 'I love you, I love you, I love you.'

Theo groaned and held her so tight that she thought she would break in two. And letting him make love to her after a period of hating him was more fulfilling than she could ever have imagined. He took her to the heavens and back and when finally he let her go, when they were both sated as only two lovers could be, she felt oddly bereft. She never, ever wanted Theo to move from her side. He was her life now.

She turned her head, looked at the man lying beside her and smiled. She hadn't realised that he was watching her through lazy lids.

'That was something, wasn't it?' he asked.

'Mmm!'

He kissed her long and hard and then looked into her eyes. 'I know I put pressure on you; I know you reluctantly married me and couldn't wait for our contract to end, but as I said before I knew from the moment I set eyes on you that you were destined to be my wife. One way or another I would have captured your heart.'

'It's an odd way of doing it,' she mused. 'Marrying first and falling in love second. What if we hadn't fallen in love, what if there had been no baby? Do you think we would have been able to walk away?'

'We'll never know,' said Theo.

But Dione did. She hadn't been aware of it at the time, it was only now that realisation dawned, but she too had fallen in love with Theo right from the word go. She'd used the pretext of marrying him for her father's sake, but deep down inside something must have told her that he was her destiny.

She smiled. 'No, Theo! We'll never know.'

EPILOGUE

'WHAT did you say, Mother?' Dione had phoned her mother every week since Yannis' death, but she'd had no inkling that anything had changed in Jeannie's life.

'I said I'm going to get married again.'

Dione held her hand over the receiver and turned to Theo where he sat cradling their baby. 'My mother's going to get married.'

He grinned and stuck his thumb up. And Dione had never seen him look more content. He adored their son and wasn't afraid to show it.

'You never said you had a boyfriend, Mother.'

'I was scared in case it didn't last. But I think I've finally shaken off your father's ghost and I'm ready to live my life again.'

'Good for you,' said Dione fervently. 'When am I going to meet this lucky man?'

'I thought we'd fly over for Easter. If that's OK with you?'

'It's more than OK,' cried Dione. 'Oh, Mother, I'm so happy for you.' There had been a time when her mother wouldn't set foot in Greece, but now she had become a regular visitor and Dione had never been happier.

And Phrosini too was getting on with her life. She had thrown herself with gusto into running Yannis' restaurant business and things were looking up at last.

'Isn't he the most beautiful baby you've ever seen?' Dione put down the phone and perched on the arm of Theo's chair, looking at her son adoringly. Leander looked just like his father and she was happier than ever.

'Naturally,' agreed Theo. 'Any baby of yours would be beautiful.'

He had become a doting father-to-be over the last few months, treating Dione like a princess, showing her in every way possible how much he loved her. And he seemed to have got over his paranoia about losing Nikos. He was already planning for their baby's future, and the future of those who were not yet even a twinkle in his eye. Dione could see that she'd have her time cut out looking after all of Theo's babies.

Not that it would be any real hardship. He'd already employed a nanny, much against Dione's wishes, and he was prepared to employ a whole army of helpers if it eased the load of his princess.

'You're wasting your money,' she protested time and time again, but he took no notice. He simply smiled and did whatever he wanted to do.

And when Leander was seven months old Dione found herself pregnant again.

'We really will have to stop doing this,' she said to Theo as they lay exhausted in each other's arms a few evenings later.

'Don't you enjoy making babies?' he asked with a wicked smile, stroking her hair back from her damp forehead.

Dione grinned. 'It's the best pastime I know.'

'Then I think we should carry on until we're too old to do it.'

Dione pretended to groan. 'I think that will be for ever, my darling.'

'Then so be it,' he said.

* * * * *

*Turn the page for an exclusive extract
from Harlequin Presents®*

THE PLAYBOY SHEIKH'S VIRGIN STABLE-GIRL
by
Sharon Kendrick

Claimed by the sheikh—for her innocence!

Polo-playing Sheikh Prince Kaliq Al'Farisi loves
his women as much as his horses. They're wild,
willing and he's their master!

Stable girl Eleni is a local Calistan girl. Raised by
her brutal father on the horse racing circuit, she
feels unlovable. When her precious horses are given
to Sheikh Kaliq she *refuses* to be parted from them.

The playboy sheikh is determined to bed her, and
when he realizes she's a virgin the challenge only
becomes more interesting. However, Kaliq is
torn; his body wants Eleni, yet his heart wants to
protect her....

"WHAT WOULD YOU SAY, MY DAUGHTER, if I told you that a royal prince was coming to the home of your father?"

She would say that he *had* been drinking, after all. But never to his face, of course. If Papa was having one of his frequent flights of fancy then it was always best to play along with it.

Eleni kept her face poker-straight. "A royal prince, Papa?" she questioned gravely.

"Yes, indeed!" He pushed his face forward. "The Prince Kaliq Al'Farisi," he crowed, "is coming to my house to play cards with me!"

Her father had gone insane! These were ideas of grandeur run riot! And what was Eleni to do? What if he continued to make such idle boasts in front of the men who were sitting waiting to begin the long night of card-playing? Surely that would make him a laughing-stock and ruin what little reputation he had left.

"Papa," she whispered urgently, "I beg you to think clearly. What place would a royal prince have *here?*"

But she was destined never to hear a reply, even though his mouth had opened like a puppet's, for there came the sound of distant hooves. The steady, powerful thud of horses as they thundered over the parched sands. On the still, thick air the muffled beat grew closer and louder until it filled Eleni's ears like the sound of the desert wolves that howled at the silver moon when it was at its fullest.

Toward them galloped a clutch of four horses, and as Eleni watched, one of them broke free and surged forward like a black stream of oil gushing out of the arid sand. For a moment, she stood there, transfixed—for this was as beautiful and as reckless a piece of riding as she had ever witnessed.

Illuminated by the orange-gold of the dying sun, she saw a colossus of a man with an ebony stallion between his thighs that he urged on with a joyful shout. The man's bare head was as dark as the horse he rode and his skin gleamed like some bright and burnished metal. Robes of pure silk clung to the hard sinews of his body. As he approached, Eleni could see a face so forbidding that some deep-rooted fear made her wonder if he had the power to turn to dust all those who stood before him.

And a face so inherently beautiful that it was as if all the desert flowers had bloomed at once.

It was then that Eleni understood the full and daunting truth. Her father's bragging *had* been true, and riding toward their humble abode was indeed Prince Kaliq Al'Farisi. Kaliq the daredevil, the lover of women, the playboy, the gambler and irresponsible twin son of Prince Ashraf. The man it was said could make women moan with pleasure simply by looking at them.

She had not seen him since she was a young girl in the crowds watching the royal family pass by. Back then, he had been doing his military service and wearing the uniform of the Calistan Navy. And back then he had been an arresting young man, barely out of his twenties. But now—a decade and a half on—he was at the most magnificent peak of his manhood, with a raw and beautiful masculinity that seemed to shimmer from his muscular frame.

"By the wolves that howl!" Eleni whimpered, and ran inside the house.

* * * * *

Be sure to look for
THE PLAYBOY SHEIKH'S VIRGIN STABLE-GIRL
by Sharon Kendrick,
available August 2009 from Harlequin Presents®!

HARLEQUIN *Presents*

TWO CROWNS, TWO ISLANDS, ONE LEGACY

A royal family torn apart by pride and lust for power, reunited by purity and passion

THE ROYAL HOUSE *of* KAREDES

Pick up the next adventure in this passionate series!

THE PLAYBOY SHEIKH'S VIRGIN STABLE-GIRL
by Sharon Kendrick, August 2009

THE PRINCE'S CAPTIVE WIFE
by Marion Lennox, September 2009

THE SHEIKH'S FORBIDDEN VIRGIN
by Kate Hewitt, October 2009

THE GREEK BILLIONAIRE'S INNOCENT PRINCESS
by Chantelle Shaw, November 2009

THE FUTURE KING'S LOVE-CHILD
by Melanie Milburne, December 2009

RUTHLESS BOSS, ROYAL MISTRESS
by Natalie Anderson, January 2010

THE DESERT KING'S HOUSEKEEPER BRIDE
by Carol Marinelli, February 2010

Eight volumes to collect and treasure!

ROYAL AND RUTHLESS

Royally bedded, regally wedded!

A Mediterranean majesty, a Greek prince, a desert
king and a fierce nobleman—with any of these men
around, a royal bedding is imminent!

And when they're done in the bedroom, the next
thing to arrange is a very regal wedding!

**Look for all of these fabulous stories
available in August 2009!**

Innocent Mistress, Royal Wife #65
by ROBYN DONALD

The Ruthless Greek's Virgin Princess #66
by TRISH MOREY

The Desert King's Bejewelled Bride #67
by SABRINA PHILIPS

Veretti's Dark Vengeance #68
by LUCY GORDON

REQUEST YOUR FREE BOOKS!

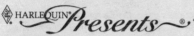

2 FREE NOVELS
PLUS 2
FREE GIFTS!

YES! Please send me 2 FREE Harlequin Presents® novels and my 2 FREE gifts (gifts are worth about $10). After receiving them, if I don't wish to receive any more books, I can return the shipping statement marked "cancel". If I don't cancel, I will receive 6 brand-new novels every month and be billed just $4.05 per book in the U.S. or $4.74 per book in Canada. That's a savings of close to 15% off the cover price! It's quite a bargain! Shipping and handling is just 50¢ per book*. I understand that accepting the 2 free books and gifts places me under no obligation to buy anything. I can always return a shipment and cancel at any time. Even if I never buy another book, the two free books and gifts are mine to keep forever.

106 HDN EYRQ 306 HDN EYR2

Name	(PLEASE PRINT)	
Address		Apt. #
City	State/Prov.	Zip/Postal Code

Signature (if under 18, a parent or guardian must sign)

Mail to the **Harlequin Reader Service:**
IN U.S.A.: P.O. Box 1867, Buffalo, NY 14240-1867
IN CANADA: P.O. Box 609, Fort Erie, Ontario L2A 5X3

Not valid to current subscribers of Harlequin Presents books.

Are you a current subscriber of Harlequin Presents books and want to receive the larger-print edition? Call 1-800-873-8635 today!

* Terms and prices subject to change without notice. Prices do not include applicable taxes. Sales tax applicable in N.Y. Canadian residents will be charged applicable provincial taxes and GST. Offer not valid in Quebec. This offer is limited to one order per household. All orders subject to approval. Credit or debit balances in a customer's account(s) may be offset by any other outstanding balance owed by or to the customer. Please allow 4 to 6 weeks for delivery. Offer available while quantities last.

Your Privacy: Harlequin Books is committed to protecting your privacy. Our Privacy Policy is available online at www.eHarlequin.com or upon request from the Reader Service. From time to time we make our lists of customers available to reputable third parties who may have a product or service of interest to you. If you would prefer we not share your name and address, please check here. ☐

HP09R

HARLEQUIN *Presents*®

International Billionaires

Life is a game of power and pleasure.
And these men play to win!

BLACKMAILED INTO THE GREEK TYCOON'S BED
by Carol Marinelli

When ruthless billionaire Xante Rossi catches
mousy Karin red-handed, he designs a way to save
her from scandal. But she'll have to earn
the favor—in his bedroom!

Book #2846

Available August 2009

Look for the last installment of
International Billionaires from Harlequin Presents!

THE VIRGIN SECRETARY'S IMPOSSIBLE BOSS
by Carole Mortimer
September 2009

HARLEQUIN *Presents*

NIGHTS *of* PASSION

One night is never enough!

*These guys know what they want
and how they're going to get it!*

NAUGHTY NIGHTS IN THE MILLIONAIRE'S MANSION
by **Robyn Grady**

Millionaire businessman Mitch Stuart wants no
distractions...until he meets Vanessa Craig.
Mitch will help her financially, but bewitching
Vanessa threatens his corporate rule: do not mix
business with pleasure....

Book #2850

Available August 2009

Look for more of these hot stories throughout the
year from Harlequin Presents!

HP12850